Keyed Up

Laura M. Baird

BLACK ROSE
writing™

© 2017 by Laura M. Baird

All rights reserved. No part of this book may be reproduced, stored in a retrieval system or transmitted in any form or by any means without the prior written permission of the publishers, except by a reviewer who may quote brief passages in a review to be printed in a newspaper, magazine or journal.

The final approval for this literary material is granted by the author.

First printing

This is a work of fiction. Names, characters, businesses, places, events and incidents are either the products of the author's imagination or used in a fictitious manner. Any resemblance to actual persons, living or dead, or actual events is purely coincidental.

ISBN: 978-1-61296-923-7
PUBLISHED BY BLACK ROSE WRITING
www.blackrosewriting.com

Printed in the United States of America
Suggested Retail Price (SRP) $17.95

Keyed Up is printed in Book Antiqua

Always, to my husband, Scott, whom I love with all my heart! To my family and friends – thanks for the encouragement on never giving up.

6/18

Rayanne —

Thanks so much for your support. It's been wonderful connecting with you, and I look forward to meeting you in person. Happy reading and happy writing!

Laurie Baird

Keyed Up

Chapter 1

Penelope Dixon rushed through the doors of the concert hall, raven curls bouncing around her shoulders and in her face. Her steps faltered as she swiped them away, causing her to nearly collide with a gentleman who was crossing her path.

"Whoa, Miss, careful there," he greeted her, his voice pleasantly calm.

"I'm so sorry, Sir." Penelope adjusted the strap of her satchel across her body, straightened her jacket, and tried taming her hair once again.

"Running late, are you?" He chuckled.

"Unfortunately, yes," she replied, breathless. "Not the impression I had hoped to make on my first day here."

Penelope would be making her headline debut with the Seattle Symphony in just three short weeks, and other than Maestro Frederic LaPelle, she had yet to meet anyone else associated with Benaroya Hall or the orchestra. She had unwisely ignored the recent emails regarding the current happenings with the Symphony due to her hasty move, but promised herself that she would catch up this evening.

After years of playing in the shadow of her famous father, classical pianist Bernard Dixon, she was finally stepping out into the light. And, as much as it thrilled her, she had to be honest with herself and admit that a part of her was scared silly.

Since losing her mother before her second birthday, her father had been her world. It was rare for them to be apart for more than a few days at a time. Although she had had a nanny for a period, as well as

Gertie, their beloved household manager, Bernard always made sure that he had been active in Penelope's upbringing no matter how busy his schedule seemed. His guidance and encouragement in her endeavors were backed by love; never pushing her on a course that wasn't of her own choosing. And, years ago, when Penelope's first love interest rocked her world to its core – and not in a good way – she sought comfort in remaining close to her father and being the dutiful daughter.

Imagine if you had made this choice long ago as you had yearned to do? What course would your life have taken?

Now near the age of twenty-eight, Penelope was striking out on her own as her father decided to slow down his career. No longer would she have him or the multitude of other staffers from her home in San Francisco, guiding her choices and making sure her every need was met – per Bernard's instructions of course.

Penelope hoped she had learned from that guidance, and now relished the freedom to make decisions that would be hers and hers alone.

It's past time –

Penelope was drawn out of her thoughts by the gentleman asking a question.

"I'm sorry, what did you say?"

"I asked if I may be of assistance."

An easy smile adorned the man's face, instantly putting her at ease. He reminded her of her father. From the looks of it, they were close in age. Smiling in return, she replied, "Yes, please. I'm told I'm to report to Maestro, or rather, Conductor LaPelle." Maestro was more of an honorary title; and antiquated. Music director or conductor was most commonly used. "I'm Penelope Dixon, new pianist."

"Ah, yes, I thought I'd recognized you. These old eyes aren't what they used to be." He grinned. "Well, young lady, it's an honor to meet you. I'm Henry, Henry Stanton, one of the cellists." He bowed his head in greeting. "When we heard that you'd be joining our ranks, we were all very excited."

"Thank you, Sir, I–"

"Please, call me Henry. When not in the presence of the Director, we all like to remain informal. Well, most of us do," he added with a chuckle. "I'm on my way into the recital hall where the others are gathering for practice. I'll escort you." He looped his arm through hers and began walking. "It's not often we get an esteemed musician such as yourself available so late in the season."

It was nearly mid-March, and Penelope knew the Seattle Symphony's season ran from September to July. Due to a family emergency, the previous resident pianist had been unable to complete the season, allowing Penelope to be awarded the position.

She blushed at Henry's compliment.

"Thank you, again. I must say, this is a beautiful building." As Penelope looked around, bright rays lit up the grand foyer. The warmth washed over them as they walked toward their destination. A rare sunny day had postponed the incessant dreary gray she had heard so much about in the Pacific Northwest. Penelope figured it was only a matter of time before she experienced the so-called never ending rain.

"Have you never been before now?"

"Briefly, but I was only eight at the time and barely remember. My father made an appearance here a year after it opened. Unfortunately, I took ill the night of his performance and had to remain with my nanny in our suite."

Henry nodded in understanding. "I've only recently joined the Symphony myself. Never in your years of touring did you return?"

"Astonishingly, no." Penelope chuckled. "Much of my touring with my father was international. I've played in San Francisco, as well as on the East Coast a handful of times. I'm very much looking forward to playing here."

"My dear, you are in for a treat." Henry continued to guide Penelope through the building and into the recital hall, the smaller of the two auditoria within the building. Roughly eighty people were milling about, setting up their stands, and tuning or practicing on their instruments. A variety of notes, chords, and scales tickled Penelope's ears – a welcomed sound indeed.

Henry led Penelope directly to the grand piano that sat front and center of the musicians. He raised his arm, and before she knew what was happening, the cymbalist crashed his cymbals together, startling most, especially Penelope herself. Henry comforted her with a pat on the arm.

"My fellow musicians," Henry began, his melodious voice conquering the quiet. "May I introduce to you, Penelope Dixon, our new pianist."

Once again, Penelope blushed as the applause and murmurs of welcome began. Knowing she hadn't the voice that Henry did, she simply bowed and smiled to the room.

"I didn't mean to embarrass you, my dear. Please, get accustomed to your new seat." He indicated the bench in front of the piano. "I believe the piano was just tuned this weekend, so it should be ready for you."

Penelope nodded as she eyed the black beauty that was the Steinway. It gleamed as if brand new; the polish remarkable and the ivories a brilliant white. The bench beckoned, inviting her to sit on the plush cushion. She couldn't control the grin that spread across her face as she lightly ran her finger tips along the side of the piano, its surface smooth as glass and cool to the touch. Once at the bench, she removed her satchel then her jacket, placing them on the floor beside her. Scooting the seat out to adjust for her sitting position, she made herself comfortable. She feathered the keys, eager to disturb them, knowing that was exactly what this masterpiece was made for; to produce incomparable sound.

Penelope was instantly in her own little world, heedless of the others in the room. Her full concentration was on the connection she was going to make with this instrument. She ran a few scales, testing the resistance of the keys and strings along with the foot pedals. Once satisfied with the feel, she started to play Rachmaninov Piano Concerto No. 2. It began with tentative strikes to the keys, building in volume and speed. Before she knew it, many of the members had joined in, adding their exquisite sound. They were completely in sync, the absence of the conductor making no difference.

In a matter of moments, Penelope became lost in the music, unaware of the audience that had gathered in the darkened rows in the back.

Laura M. Baird

—

Sebastian Mauer sat with the Symphony's music director, LaPelle, witnessing the performance of one Penelope Dixon. While he knew the man was evaluating her fundamentals, her timing, her accuracy with the music, he was not. Well, not entirely. Yes, her fundamentals were important, as they were the basis for her play; the foundation that all great players needed to have. But what held his attention was the absolute passion with which she played. He had seen her perform over the years, but it didn't compare to what she had fully developed into.

Penelope's fingers flew across the keys, the piano becoming an extension of the woman herself. The magnificent sound that emanated from it nearly took his breath away. And that in itself was something of a rarity.

He watched the flawless movements of her hands and feet. Although her eyes were now closed, he knew they were blue. When she opened them, they dazzled. Her face danced with expression, her head moving in fluid motion to the tempo. At one point, she threw her head back and smiled radiantly, causing her entire being to light up. Even with her seated, Sebastian could make out the willowy form of her body. Her leggings outlined the graceful lines of her legs, stopping mid-calf to expose her slender ankles. She wore a sweater atop her leggings and black flats adorned her feet.

Sebastian was so caught up in watching Penelope that he didn't even notice when LaPelle left his side to walk towards the musicians. It wasn't until he took his position behind the podium and began rapping on it to silence the group that Sebastian was startled out of his concentration. He heard Penelope fumble with the music, clearly startled herself. She scrambled from the bench, nearly tipping it over in the process. Her posture was ramrod straight with her hands clasped in front of her as LaPelle began to speak.

He almost felt sorry for her.

Cursing himself for his feelings, he wasn't surprised that this beautiful creature had once again stirred his soul; and in no less than thirty minutes.

Sebastian was here out of obligation to Bernard Dixon. Once a world renowned performer in the symphony circuit himself, Sebastian now preferred a more sedate lifestyle out of the limelight. He excelled at composing, and thanks to Bernard, a selection of his pieces had become a staple at many symphony halls, propelling Sebastian's composing career.

Now, after many years of limited contact, Bernard was calling in on the unspoken debt, thinking that a collaboration between Sebastian and Penelope would be stupendous. He requested that Sebastian say nothing of his manipulation in his daughter's career. Penelope hadn't a clue about her father using his influence in gaining her the position here at the Symphony. After all, Bernard felt justified since his intentions were done purely out of love.

Sebastian was leery to say the least. After falling in love with Penelope years ago and foolishly pushing her away, she had relentlessly occupied his thoughts and dreams. The guilt of his actions haunted him, and even worse was the deception towards Bernard for having kept his love for Penelope a secret from his mentor; his friend.

Little did Sebastian realize that Bernard had known all along.

His first thought after listening to Bernard's request was to say no, because enduring the nearness of Penelope without being able to rekindle their love would be pure torture. Who was he to think he deserved another chance? They'd had no contact for nearly ten years. Surely she must have moved on? The thought had Sebastian's insides curdling before he shoved it aside. What little he was able to garner from the abysmal amount of press on Penelope gave no hint to any relationships.

After Bernard's incessant pleading, Sebastian resigned himself to fulfill this obligation to his dear friend and be done. He'd keep this relationship strictly professional and not cause her another moment of pain.

But looking at her now, he wondered what her voice would be like whispering in his ear. What would her hands feel like, playing across his body with such passion as she just displayed at the piano? How would her body feel pressed underneath the weight of his?

You're a true glutton for punishment.

Sebastian groaned, silently cursing himself twice over for such thoughts. At this point in their lives, their ten year age difference wasn't a concern, but he still viewed her as the innocent daughter of his friend and he'd be damned if he'd cross that line again.

He had the desire.

He hadn't the right.

Chapter 2

Penelope gasped and nearly toppled the bench when she struggled to stand. Director LaPelle tapped relentlessly on the podium to silence the musicians. Who else would dare pick up the conductor's baton and stand at his sacred perch?

"Good morning, Ms. Dixon," he greeted.

Maestro Frederic LaPelle was a lean, small-statured man; but no less commanding. Salt and pepper hair graced his head in a thickness that many, at his age of sixty or even younger, would be envious of. Penelope had often heard many a praise about the man's warmth and congeniality from her father; although at the moment, his grey eyes held no hint of anything other than annoyance.

Whatever did I do to earn that look?

"G-good morning, Maestro LaPelle. I was just warming up." She nervously glanced around. "And the others–"

"Were kind enough to join in," he finished. "Yes, so I gathered. If it's quite all right with you, I'd say it's time to get down to business."

"Yes, sir. Ready, sir."

"We shall see, won't we?"

"Yes we shall," she mumbled to herself.

"Do you have something to add, Ms. Dixon?"

"Not at all, Sir."

He abruptly nodded and turned to the orchestra, clearly dismissing her and instructing the others to prepare themselves. "We will begin with the performance of Mozart's Piano Concerto No. 22. Ms. Dixon, do you require sheet music?"

"No sir," she stated flatly. Penelope was well familiar with the piece, having performed it numerous times on stage.

"Very well, take your seat and let's begin."

Penelope seated herself once again at the piano. The orchestra began its intro, and nearly two and half minutes into the piece, Penelope began. Eyes open, concentrating, both hands manipulating the keys. Then one hand at the higher keys. Then two hands again. The orchestra became backdrop to her, the rhythm with which to set her own course. Her fingers flew, slowed, teased, caressed, flew again. Over and over it went for nearly thirty-three minutes.

When the piece concluded, many of the members of the orchestra actually stood and cheered for Penelope. She returned their enthusiasm by standing, bowing, and clapping her hands for them. LaPelle quickly killed the joyous spirit by rapping against the podium once again.

"That was adequate for your first trial, Ms. Dixon." He barely glanced her way. "I'll provide the complete itinerary of the practice schedule as well as the pieces we'll be playing. You'll see me directly after our rehearsal."

Before she could utter a response, he struck the podium again and turned his attention to the entire group. "And now, I'd like to introduce everyone to an esteemed colleague. An extraordinary musician-turned-composer who will be collaborating with us for the next three weeks, as our recent posting had hinted on. Without further ado, please welcome, Sebastian Mauer!" LaPelle raised an arm toward the back of the room.

Penelope gasped, nearly choking on her surprise. Thankfully with the applause from the rest of the orchestra, her reaction went unnoticed. She turned toward the seats, hoping to quickly regain her composure. Out of the darkness, she watched as the emerging figure took on an all-too-familiar form.

"Bastian," she whispered.

The cliché ran through her mind – as much as things change, they remain the same. Sebastian Mauer still held himself with masculine poise and confidence, capturing everyone's attention in an instant, but he had definitely evolved into something much more; a devastatingly handsome man who looked more at ease with himself than he had years before.

As he calmly approached the group, a humble smile lit up his face. A face that now sported a short, neatly groomed beard and mustache. *The look suits him well*, Penelope thought.

Sebastian was dressed casually in khakis and a button-up shirt, long sleeves rolled up to his elbows. Dark brown hair pushed back from his face fell just below his ears. She thought his sea green eyes might avoid her altogether as his gaze swept across the group. Her breath caught when he pinned her with a heated stare. It lasted all of a few seconds, but it may as well have lasted hours. He quickly turned away and came to a halt at LaPelle's podium.

Penelope's heart beat frantically in her chest, her breathing increased to near panting.

Don't make a fool of yourself. Composure, composure, composure, she repeated to herself. Then Sebastian's rich voice rang out, feeling like a caress across her senses.

"Thank you, thank you. It's a great pleasure to be here and work with such a wonderful group. And may I also welcome Penelope Dixon, as I understand this will be her debut with the symphony."

Penelope was startled at his words but should not have been surprised at the deflection of attention off of him. Heat infused her face and her pulse quickened even more as another round of applause began. She glanced at Sebastian, catching a hint of a smile from him before she bowed her head. Staring at him any longer would probably cause her to swoon, and wouldn't that be embarrassing?

"Yes, yes," LaPelle began. "We are fortunate to have the talents of both you and Ms. Dixon. We are especially fortunate to have the opportunity to debut your latest composition." Before murmurs of excitement could get carried away, he continued. "I have copies of the music for everyone which I'll begin passing out in a moment. So as not to waste a minute of precious time, given that our first performance is less than three weeks away, we'll begin to familiarize ourselves with the music. If I could have the first chairs from each section come up please."

Penelope was at a loss as to what to do next. Should she approach Sebastian and LaPelle? She longed to speak with him, but was petrified at the same time. It had been over nine years since she last laid eyes on him. Anger and delight warred with one another.

She felt overwhelmed and feared a panic attack was oncoming.

Penelope closed her eyes and took a calming breath. When she opened them, Henry approached and saved her from any monumental decisions at the moment.

"My dear, you were marvelous. And you handled yourself extremely well under the pressure of the Maestro." He winked, using the title she had used earlier. "He likes you."

"Are you joking? If that was a display of him liking me, I'd hate to see what he'd do if he disliked me."

"If that were the case, you'd have never been invited to join us, nor allowed a seat at the Steinway."

Penelope gasped and whirled around when LaPelle spoke out from behind her. Her cheeks burned in embarrassment.

Turning toward Henry, LaPelle handed him several copies of the music. "For you and your section." He then turned his attention back to Penelope. "And here is your copy of the composition. Welcome, Penelope Dixon." He handed her the music and gave her a brief smile. Suddenly, he hid his face in the crook of his arm and let out a sneeze.

"Bless you," Penelope said automatically.

"Thank you," he returned. "Allergies." He began to walk away while pulling a handkerchief from his pocket.

Penelope stared down at the sheets in front of her, unable to believe that she held Sebastian's work in her hands. Literally. A niggling in her brain had her looking up and her vision collided with the man that was suddenly consuming her thoughts.

—

Conflicting emotions ran amuck through Sebastian's mind. Elation. Fear. Panic. His shield quickly dissolved like a sand castle being washed away in the surf.

He was halfway in love with her again.

Who are you kidding? Your love for her never stopped. You just pushed it away and lived in misery ever since.

Sebastian couldn't control the heat that burned deep as he watched Penelope holding his masterpiece. Unknown to her, she had been the inspiration behind his composition he had started so many years ago and only recently completed. And now, she would be making her debut playing that very piece.

As she looked up and their eyes locked, he had no choice but to make his way over to her. Needing to be near her.

You're playing with fire. Professional relationship only.
Good luck with that.

Fighting for control, he walked toward her and the cellist at her side. Her eyes widened and never left his as he drew close. Before either could speak, the older gentleman greeted him.

"Mr. Mauer, such an honor to meet you. I'm Henry Stanton, first chair cellist. I know I speak for everyone in the Symphony when I say what a pleasure it will be to perform your work."

Sebastian smiled at the man and nodded his head. "Thank you very much, Henry. And please, call me Sebastian. It's my pleasure to be here." He turned his attention to Penelope, fixating on her brilliant blue eyes. "And what an honor for me, having Ms. Dixon perform my composition."

Sebastian was rewarded with her quick inhale that had her perfect lips parting and her eyes widening even more. The music sheets fluttered in her trembling hands. He desperately wanted to cover those delicate hands with his and pull her to him in order to ease the apparent nervousness she was feeling.

Realizing that Henry was speaking, he turned his attention back to the gentleman.

"Again, a pleasure. If you'll excuse me, I'll make sure my section gets their music. I'll let you and Penelope become acquainted." Henry nodded his head to each of them before walking away.

The silence seemed deafening as Sebastian and Penelope faced one another, neither speaking. He made no effort to hide his study of her as his gaze wandered over the lush curls that framed her face and hovered at her shoulders. Her eyes held more maturity, yet still seemed so innocent at the same time. Her creamy skin glowed even with no makeup, allowing for her natural beauty to shine. Her lips remained parted as if on the verge of saying something. Sebastian longed to lean in and capture them with his own. He longed to relearn the softness of her neck and linger above her collarbone.

Would it still drive her wild to have my lips suckling that spot?

He wanted to continue his perusal down the rest of her body, but her timid words brought him out of his own thoughts.

"Hello, Sebastian," she said softly.

"Hello, Penelope. You look lovely."

Sebastian enjoyed the blush that crept into her cheeks. The action immediately sent his own blood raging through him and bringing to life a certain part of his anatomy, that if he didn't get under control soon, he'd have great difficulty hiding.

"Thank you. You're looking quite well yourself," she stated mechanically, as if it were her duty to be pleasant. "What a surprise. I had no idea you'd be working with the Symphony."

"Yes, well, it was literally a last-minute decision, having received the call a few weeks ago. Luckily, I had just finished my new piece and felt it worthy." He cocked his head, analyzing her cool demeanor. "I take it you still avoid reading anything extraneous. Didn't Frederic inform you of my collaboration?" When she raised a brow at him, he continued. "I suppose I shouldn't be so informal by using the director's first name. He does prefer LaPelle, after all. Surely you got his email?"

"I'm sure I did, but I have been very lax on catching up with my emails, and–"

Her words were cut short by the director calling for everyone to take their positions and prepare for rehearsal.

"Looks like it's time to get to work," he said.

"Yes, well, I suppose you should have the honor." She stepped away from the bench, indicating that he take the seat in order to play. Again, LaPelle's words halted her movement and clearly surprised her.

"Ms. Dixon, please join Mr. Mauer at the bench so that you'll have the opportunity to follow the music this first time through."

Sebastian couldn't have been more pleased, but it was evident by Penelope's hesitation that she didn't feel the same way.

He drew near to her and whispered, "Please join me."

Sebastian could admit his enjoyment in watching her body visibly shiver.

Chapter 3

Penelope tried to control her body's tremor at Sebastian's request. She took a deep breath and his scent filled her; crisp and clean, with a hint of mint. She remembered that he loved to keep gum in his mouth, not necessarily chewing it the entire time, but mostly rolling it around to keep his mouth moist. That memory and his nearness sent a delightful zing through her body. Before said body could further betray her, she breathed again, relaxed, and silently thanked her yoga instructor for the many sessions over the years.

Smiling before leaning forward, Penelope placed the music sheets on the piano. Sebastian waited for her to be seated before sitting next to her. The brush of his wide shoulders sent a heated frisson along her nerve endings, and once again her control was at risk of being lost. She nearly leapt off the bench, desperately wanting more space between them. In the next thought she desperately wanted him to surround her with his strong arms and reignite what started so many years ago.

Don't be a fool. He ended it and never contacted you again. He obviously moved on.

Penelope wasn't given any more time for self-reflection as LaPelle struck the podium with three short taps. He nodded to Sebastian who began his intro without the orchestra. Penelope followed the music as Sebastian expertly worked the keys for a haunting opening that lasted nearly five minutes. One by one, sections of the symphony joined in as instructed, and the piece quickened to a livelier tempo. The orchestra did remarkably well considering they had just laid eyes on the music.

For nearly thirty minutes it went and Penelope felt the joy and the uplifting spirit of the piece. Her heart raced, her skin tingled; she felt her cheeks tighten with her broad smile.

Until the end.

The piece came to a crashing, tumultuous halt that startled Penelope. The final strikes to the piano sounded as if broken glass was raining down. The hall became deadly silent as Penelope felt Sebastian's gaze on her. She turned to look at him, her eyes moist, threatening to spill over. Try as she might, she couldn't ascertain his emotions.

His eyes seemed to soften with sadness, sympathy... regret?

Just as Penelope was about to speak, LaPelle shouted. "Marvelous!"

As members of the orchestra began applauding, Sebastian looked away from Penelope and began clapping himself. He stood and addressed the group. "Thank you. You were *all* marvelous. I'm even more eager now to hear Ms. Dixon's rendition."

"Indeed," LaPelle said. "Why don't we see just what she's capable of? Ms. Dixon, if you'd be so kind as to get comfortable, we'll run through the piece again with you at the helm."

"Yes, sir." Penelope quickly swiped her eyes with her hands and rubbed them across her leggings. After a quick inhale, she situated herself on the bench before Sebastian returned to his position beside her. Taking a moment to seemingly study the music before beginning, she only now realized the piece was simply titled, "Composition - 2/17".

Interesting. Had he no time to properly name it, or had –

Sebastian subtly cleared his throat, bringing Penelope back to the task at hand. Aware that everyone was waiting on her, she poised her hands above the piano, took a deep breath, and began. Penelope blocked out everything around her while she focused on the music, making the keys dance beneath her fingers. She paid no mind to the fact that it was Sebastian's hands that turned the pages, for she had already memorized the piece. A gift that most found astounding.

Immersing herself in the composition, she imagined a story being plotted out. A lonely soul; wandering, searching. For what? Suddenly, light breaks through the dark and a joyous spirit surrounds the soul.

Keyed Up

There is happiness, hope. But unfortunately, it doesn't last. That happiness is ripped away, cast aside. By choice? Or beyond means of control? The soul is broken, lost again...heart shattered into pieces.

After striking the final notes, Penelope's head hung forward, tears coating her face. She took a shuddering breath before she raised her head. The silence of the hall was overwhelming, but before she could think too long on that, she was startled by a thunderous applause as the entire Symphony stood.

Penelope blinked once, twice, her gaze drawn toward Sebastian.

"That is for you," he whispered.

Before she could comprehend his meaning, LaPelle seemed to clap the loudest as he spoke. "Ms. Dixon, words cannot do justice to what you just gave us. My dear, I cannot *wait* for opening night!"

Penelope had the presence of mind to stand as she smiled and bowed to the group. Noticing that Sebastian had extended his hand to offer her a handkerchief, she could only stare, surprised by his action. When she didn't move, he took her hand and pressed the cloth to her palm. His warm skin shocked but somehow comforted as she clutched the fabric tightly before wiping her face.

"Thank you," she murmured.

As the applause quieted, LaPelle once again addressed the group. "I think with that, we'll actually adjourn for the day and pick up tomorrow at nine. Everyone, please study the music and check your email tonight for an updated itinerary. There's also an announcement about a reception this Friday, the details of which will be in the email.

"Sebastian, Ms. Dixon, please join me in my office."

Without waiting for an answer, LaPelle gathered his papers from the podium and walked toward the exit. As the other musicians began packing away their instruments, Penelope quickly swiped at her eyes again before standing from the bench to retrieve her items. Sebastian pulled the cover down over the keys on the piano and took the music sheets in his hands.

"I believe this is yours," he said.

Penelope reluctantly faced Sebastian, staring only at his hand that offered the music, knowing full well she couldn't bear to have him see her in this state; eyes glossy, emotions raw. Without looking at him, she reached out to take the sheets. Surprise caused her to gasp when his free hand gently cradled hers and she had no choice but to meet his gaze. She thought she saw kindness, patience, even a flash of longing, but maybe that was wishful thinking – the kind of thinking that had no business invading her mind. When she tried to pull away, he held strong for a moment before placing the music in her hand and reluctantly withdrawing his own.

"Penelope, I–"

"We probably shouldn't keep the director waiting." She immediately turned, and in her haste nearly toppled over the bench. Sebastian was quick to steady her, bringing her close to his body. Everything seemed to fade into oblivion except for Sebastian's handsome face so close to hers. Penelope was vaguely aware of the commotion around her as members of the symphony shuffled out of the hall; her focus solely on Sebastian. His fathomless eyes as they held her attention. The rise and fall of his chest as his breathing seemed to increase. The warmth of his touch as it permeated her skin through her sweater.

Sebastian's lips were but a breath away. How easy it would be to tip her face up and meet him for a long-awaited kiss. How she longed to savor that touch; and so much more.

Reality came crashing back into focus when someone cleared their throat. Sebastian's hands released her as he took a step back, and it took all the strength Penelope had not to crumble at his feet.

Henry stood before them with a younger gal at his side. "Penelope, Sebastian, let me praise you both. What an outstanding composition you've graced us with." Turning to his companion, he went on. "Penelope, I wanted to introduce Lindsay Clarke, one of our flautists. She's very near to your age and I thought it may help to develop a friendship."

Penelope's gaze toggled from one to the other. "Thank you, Henry. Lindsay, it's certainly a pleasure meeting you, as I have yet to meet anyone other than Henry so far." Aware that Sebastian bristled beside her, seeing as they had technically already met, she steeled herself against feeling any pity for him. "If you have time, I'd love to meet with you after I've met with Director LaPelle."

The lovely young lady who had the defining features of a ginger – rich auburn hair and a smattering of freckles across her face and exposed skin – blushed and grinned. "That'd be great. If you'd like, I can wait here in the hall until you're done."

"Yes, that'd be great," Penelope echoed. "I'll see you soon." She gathered her items and proceeded to step around to clear herself from the bench and the piano; from Sebastian. "Thank you, Henry. I very much look forward to working with you. With everyone."

The gentleman nodded. "As do we, look forward to working with you. Both you and Sebastian. I'll see you in the morning. Have a pleasant evening."

"You do the same," Sebastian said, just as Penelope answered with "You as well."

As Henry turned to leave, Penelope rushed behind him, eager to separate herself from the man who jumbled her nerves, but Sebastian was quick to follow, maintaining a respectable distance behind her.

Once they all cleared the exit of the recital hall, Henry went toward another exit as Penelope came to a stop just outside the door, realizing she had no idea where LaPelle's office was. She gasped when Sebastian's quiet voice seemed to reach out and stroke her.

"If you trust me to lead the way, I'll take us to LaPelle's office."

All Penelope could do was nod. And as Sebastian strode forward, she had no choice but to follow.

Chapter 4

She can barely tolerate your presence, let alone trust you. And who could blame her?

Sebastian wished for so many things, most of all for the ability to take away the hurt he had caused Penelope. Whether or not she still harbored any feelings for him was something to which he shouldn't be giving thought. He had no right to think there was anything other than anger and distrust.

Served him right.

As he led them through a corridor towards LaPelle's office, he was entirely too aware of her presence behind him. The soft shuffle of her footsteps, the crinkling of the music sheets she still clutched to her chest instead of tucking them in her satchel, and the subtle scent of flowers…or was it peaches that he detected? Whatever it was, it was distinctly Penelope as it teased his nostrils, increased his heart beat, and made his thoughts wander.

Before Sebastian could take another breath, he was at LaPelle's door. He stopped so suddenly that he thought he'd have to brace Penelope from crashing in to him. But as he turned, she halted a few steps away.

"We're here." Sebastian rapped on the door and LaPelle's voice called out from the other side, advising them to enter. Sebastian pushed open the door and indicated for Penelope to enter first. Once she did, he followed and closed the door. The office wasn't much bigger than 10x10, with a desk and chair, a filing cabinet, and folding chairs against the wall.

"Sebastian, Ms. Dixon, please, help yourselves to a seat," he indicated to the folding chairs. "Forgive the tight quarters, but space is limited at this time due to some minor renovations."

Sebastian moved first, opening a chair and offering it to Penelope. She didn't voice a thank you, only nodded her head before taking a seat. He then repeated the process for himself. He would've given Penelope more room, knowing how uncomfortable she already felt, but with the limited space, they practically rubbed elbows. Not that he'd complain.

"Thank you for coming," LaPelle said, breaking the silence. His voice was raspy, his eyes watery; much different than only moments ago at rehearsal. "As you are both aware, we have technically less than three weeks before our next performances, the first weekend of April, and another two weeks after that. And, although today's first practice of Sebastian's piece was astounding, there's still much to do." LaPelle shuffled papers as he spoke, appearing to organize as much as he could. "Now, I'm composing the email to inform the members of the order of pieces we'll be performing, the practice schedule, as well as the announcement for the gathering Friday evening. Our calendar is set for the remainder of the season, so rehearsals will follow accordingly." He stopped to look up at the pair. "Are there any limitations to your schedule that I should be aware of?"

If LaPelle's question came as a surprise to Penelope, she showed no signs of it. Sebastian was a bit taken aback himself, given that usually the director set the schedule and there was no debate.

"Sebastian, you look surprised," LaPelle said, as if reading his mind.

He chuckled. "Yes. I suppose I'd assumed you'd set the schedule and that was that."

"Well, I have been known to be flexible. From time to time," he added with a grin. "I realize this collaboration is out of the norm for you, and I want to show my appreciation by being as accommodating as I can. There are, however, some requests I have that I'd like to run by you. Both of you," he said as he shifted his gaze to Penelope.

"Sir, my time is your time. I am completely dedicated to whatever is needed to make myself worthy and to make our performances the best that the audience could hope for."

LaPelle nodded to Penelope. "And I thank you, my dear. I had hoped that this career step for you wouldn't prove to be too much. Although your career with your father was extraordinary, it's a whole other animal, so to speak, when one becomes the headliner."

Sebastian sensed Penelope's posture tensing.

"I assure you that I am more than ready for this career step, Director LaPelle. Not to sound conceited, but my past performances were always met with high praise. I strive to give my best, not only with my technical skill, but with my heart and soul as well. I will make the Seattle Symphony proud."

"I don't think there's any doubt of that," Sebastian interjected, feeling as if he had to come to her rescue. "This morning's performances were a testament to that. I doubt that even Bernard could have done better."

At Penelope's quick inhale and wide-eyed look toward Sebastian, he backpedaled so as not to sound offending.

"What I meant to say was that–"

Luckily, LaPelle came to *his* rescue. "I think we know you meant no offense toward Penelope's father, whose career has been more than exemplary. You were merely praising her for her extraordinary talent as well and I whole-heartedly agree." He turned to Penelope. "Regardless of Bernard's influence, you would have gained the position as our pianist."

Penelope gasped and faced LaPelle with a startled expression. The man had no idea he had unintentionally ratted out her father. "You mean to say that my father is responsible for me being here? That I did not earn the seat by my own merit?"

LaPelle's gaze softened and his demeanor relaxed as he addressed her. "My dear, you are by all rights your own person, and one of the finest pianists I have had the privilege to encounter. It did not matter in the least what your father had to say, you were the only choice I would have considered. I apologize for my earlier abruptness or undue comments. Sometimes certain actions are more of a test than is required. Contrary to the notion that all maestros are prigs," he paused for a moment to chuckle. "I'm inclined to believe that I have more heart than that, and I will treat you with the respect that is both equally deserved and earned.

"Being a father myself, I can understand your father only wanting the best for you. It is a difficult situation when one realizes they must let go and allow their child to walk a path of their own. Do not berate your father for his love and concern."

Sebastian glanced from LaPelle to Penelope and watched a hesitant smile transform her lovely face. "I thank you very much, sir. I will try to understand my father's position and his actions. As for my performance here, I won't disappoint."

"I know you won't. Now, back to my question about any limitations in your schedules. Sebastian?"

Before Sebastian could answer, LaPelle let out a string of sneezes. He grabbed tissues from a nearby box and began blowing his nose. "Pardon me."

"Bless you," both Penelope and Sebastian said simultaneously.

"Thank you. Unfortunately, my allergies have come on full force." Once he disposed of the tissues and used antibacterial gel on his hands, he turned to Sebastian, awaiting an answer.

"Uh, no, there's nothing limiting that comes to mind." *The fact that I'm completely enraptured by this woman beside me should have no bearing whatsoever.*

"Good. So, about Friday evening. The Symphony Foundation has arranged for the reception to be held nearby at Tulio's Ristorante. Starting at seven, there will be drinks and hors d'oeuvres. It's a chance for the symphony members to mingle with the foundation, administrators, and socialites who support them and Benaroya Hall. Dress will not be formal, given the short notice of the announcement, nor will attendance be mandatory. Again, given the short notice.

"However," LaPelle hastily continued, "It is imperative that you be there, Sebastian, as our guest collaborator. In fact, I'm going to appeal to you further, and request that you and Penelope consent to an interview tomorrow evening."

Sebastian felt Penelope's gaze on him, and it took all he had not to look over at her, almost wishing he saw sympathy on her face for him. It's not as if he couldn't do interviews, it's just that he didn't want to. Many of the press and media almost always found a way to twist words and scenarios, or take things out of context. He'd had first-hand experience with that in the past, and the last thing he wanted right now was to have anything disrupt not only his preferred lifestyle out of the media spotlight, but also Penelope's step toward furthering her own career. He was probably overreacting, but he didn't want to take any chances.

Before he could voice his hesitation, LaPelle went on with his appeal. "Now I know your opinion of the media and your abhorrence for much of their work."

"I wouldn't term it so harshly." Sebastian couldn't help but wrinkle his nose, wondering if his view had always manifested so negatively. "I do realize that the press is needed for the support of the arts as well as the artists. I just prefer to have as much control over the process as possible."

"Certainly," LaPelle stated as he nodded his head in understanding. "Although we've done our usual advertising already, more certainly couldn't hurt. After all, it's not every day that the famed reclusive composer, Sebastian Mauer, surfaces for such an event. Every newspaper, magazine, and news station has been understandably eager to get a piece of the pie. That's why I've been able to control the situation by choosing the interviewer, and I can guarantee her credibility. Her ethics are above reproach and her stories are of high quality. I've taken the liberty of booking reservations for dinner tomorrow evening at the Fairmont for you and Ms. Dixon to meet with her. Her name is Kimberly Beacham and she's writing for the Seattle Magazine. The article will go both to print as well as on their website. Social media is all the craze, now isn't it?"

There was no mistaking LaPelle's sarcasm. Like Sebastian, he was a product of what many today would consider the 'back in the day' generation, preferring print; something tangible he could hold in his hands. Sure, Sebastian could navigate the web and operate his tablet and smart phone, and yes, sometimes those avenues were much faster, but he didn't let technology rule his life. He didn't participate in the plethora of social media outlets either.

If that made him old-fashioned in the eyes of many, so be it. He was content with his life.

But is contentment enough?

Sebastian was roused from his thoughts by Penelope's voice. "As long as you can vouch for her, and Sebastian is fine with the interview, I see no problems with it. All the more promotion for the

Symphony would be wonderful."

"Thank you for that, Ms. Dixon. Now, the dinner will be at six, if that's satisfactory."

Sebastian sat a bit stunned from Penelope's words. She actually took his feelings into consideration. *Well she's not a heartless person! What did you think she'd say? Yes, let's thrust Sebastian back into the limelight that he claims to abhor so much.*

He cleared his throat and looked at Penelope. "Yes, thank you for that, Penelope." He watched her eyes soften a fracture before she turned to face LaPelle. Sebastian turned to him as well. "Looks like we have an interview."

"Stupendous! Now, Ms. Dixon, in–"

"Apologies. Sir," Penelope interrupted. "But do you think there will come a time when you'll feel comfortable addressing me as Penelope? I would certainly have no objections to it; in fact I'd prefer it. That is if you have no objections," she nervously echoed again.

LaPelle smiled warmly. "As you wish, Penelope."

This garnered another sweet smile on Penelope's face. Oh what Sebastian wouldn't give to be the cause of that beautiful look.

LaPelle continued. "I've also emailed you both a directory of all the Symphony members. And with that, I think that that will conclude our meeting. I thank you both, again, for agreeing to the interview. I look forward to resuming our work tomorrow."

Both Sebastian and Penelope stood at the same time, saying good night to LaPelle. Once out of the office, Sebastian awkwardly faced Penelope before she could slip away. He felt the need to say… something, anything to keep her near. He realized the idiocy in that, but couldn't deny it either.

"Are you settling in okay?"

Reluctantly, it seemed, she faced him. "Yes, thank you. And you?"

"Yes. Although I miss my companions," he said automatically. At Penelope's puzzled look, he went on to explain. "Samson and Delilah, my golden retrievers."

"Really? How sweet. I–" As quick as her delight sprang forth, it disappeared even faster. "Well, I shouldn't keep Lindsay waiting. I did want to meet with her and make plans for some shopping."

"Ah yes, you ladies and your shopping," he said. He had hoped to ease the tension, but it seemed his quip only ruffled her feathers.

"Yes, we do live to shop," she said with a bite in her voice. "Because how silly of me to think I could get away with my Southern California attire in this cooler, wetter weather I'd heard so much about. Not to mention the fact that I have no attire suitable for our upcoming performances. But that's neither here nor there. And something–"

"Penelope, I apologize. I didn't mean to upset you." *Although the blush to her face was lovely, and the fire in her spirit was quite a turn-on.* "It was only in jest."

"Fine," she retorted. Her lips pinched as her brow furrowed. "Apology accepted. Now, if you'll excuse me, I should go. Good night, Sebastian."

"Good night, Penelope."

As he watched her walk away, noticing the sway of her hips and the bounce of her hair, Sebastian sighed, blowing out a frustrated breath. *Very smooth.*

Inhaling, he caught her enticing scent that lingered, further driving him insane.

"Will you ever learn?" he said to himself before turning in the opposite direction to leave.

Chapter 5

After ensuring that Sebastian hadn't followed her, Penelope leaned against the wall just outside of the recital hall where she had agreed to meet with Lindsay. She blew out a deep sigh, lifting her head to the ceiling.

"When will you learn that the less you say the better when it comes to that man?" she whispered to herself. She was still processing all that had occurred today, and all that had yet to come. Just the fact that she was reunited with Sebastian, albeit only in a professional way, had been enough to tilt her world off its axis. How would she ever survive the coming weeks being in his presence?

"You just will, because that's what you were trained to do." Penelope pushed herself away from the wall and realized she still had the sheet music clutched to her chest. Along with Sebastian's handkerchief fisted in her hand. She'd been holding them the entire time and neither LaPelle nor Sebastian thought to mention that she could tuck them away. *Good grief.* After carefully folding the sheets into her satchel and stuffing the material into her jacket pocket, she strode through the door. Lindsay was instantly on her feet, offering Penelope a gorgeous smile.

"Thank you so much for waiting for me, Lindsay. I hope you didn't have any pressing matters?"

"No, this is fine. I wouldn't have agreed to wait if I had. The only thing I need to take care of later is getting groceries and picking up my Yorkie, Aria, from the groomer's."

"All right. I'm so glad Henry introduced us. As I said, I have yet to really connect with anyone, and I was actually hoping that I could convince you to tag along with me for some shopping. I'm unfamiliar with the area and it's always more fun to have company."

"I couldn't agree more. And I would love to go shopping with you."

"Wonderful! As I was telling Se-, well as I was saying, my entire wardrobe is better suited for San Francisco, and I'm in desperate need of more formal attire. I do have some nicer outfits, but would love to acquire more. Director LaPelle just informed me that Mr. Mauer and I are having dinner with a reporter tomorrow evening," she rambled on a bit nervously. "She'll be conducting an interview on our upcoming performance. I don't suppose leggings and a loose top would work, do you?" Penelope grinned.

"Actually, it's very stylish these days, but I think we can do better. Do you need groceries also?"

"Yes, in fact, I had hoped to pick up some things that I can put in my mini fridge at the Fairmont."

"You're staying at the Fairmont Olympic Hotel?" Lindsay's excitement was palpable.

"Yes." Penelope chuckled.

"Just from the outside alone it looks fabulous. I bet it's even more so on the inside. Oh, and room service and–"

"Would you care to walk back with me? I'll give you a tour."

"I would love that! If you're sure you don't mind," Lindsay rushed on to add. "I must seem like a child."

"No. I'm giddy just knowing that I have the luxury of staying there. I admit I debated on my living accommodations, whether to find an apartment to rent or stay at someplace like the Fairmont. To be quite honest, this is the first time I've been on my own, and the last thing I wanted was to worry about cooking and cleaning. I wanted to give my full concentration to the rehearsals and preparing for the performances. Spoiled, I know," Penelope said with a laugh, her cheeks burning.

"Not at all," Lindsay countered. "If I had that opportunity, I'd take it too. I'm just lucky I have a great apartment complex that's close to the Hall. It has security and no maintenance." She winked. "Cooking and cleaning I don't mind. And it allows me to have Aria, my little Yorkie. I've had my baby for five years." The way her eyes glittered with delight, you'd think she was speaking of a child rather than a dog.

"I'd love to meet her. How about this? Let me treat you to lunch at the Fairmont, we do some shopping, and you introduce me to your baby later."

"Deal."

Penelope smiled at her new acquaintance as the two made their way out of the recital hall and into the foyer. Once they exited Benaroya Hall, they made their way two blocks up University to the Fairmont where a concierge held the door open for them. Penelope heard Lindsay's sharp intake, admiring the grand lobby with its elegant furnishings and detailed design. On the second floor was a grand piano that even now took restraint on Penelope's part not to go to it. They took their time strolling, allowing Lindsay time to take it all in. Then Penelope led them to the hotel's restaurant, The Terrace Lounge, where they were free to seat themselves.

"This," Lindsay started, "is absolutely fabulous!"

"There's more, and it's all equally fabulous. While looking through their directory, I discovered that there's a spa named *Penelope and the Beauty Bar*. How wonderful is that?" Penelope's own excitement bubbled forth. "I think you and I should definitely book some time for ourselves there."

"I've never had a spa day. That would be wonderful!"

"I thought so too. In preparation for our upcoming performance."

"We have to wait that long?" Lindsay teased.

Penelope smiled before continuing. "There's also a pool I plan to take full advantage of."

"Oh, you swim?"

Before Penelope could answer, a waitress arrived with water, and asked if they needed a minute to decide on their order.

"Actually," Penelope began, "I already know what I'd like. Do you need a minute?" she asked Lindsay.

"Go ahead and order while I take a quick look at the menu. I know what I have a taste for." As Lindsay perused the menu, Penelope placed her order of a chicken Caesar salad. It didn't take Lindsay long to follow up with her order of chicken salad sandwich on a croissant. Once the waitress left, they resumed their conversation.

"I find my release in swimming," Penelope said. "I swam competitively for a few years, but with the majority of my concentration being on my music, I couldn't devote the time and energy to swimming that I normally would give all my pursuits. So now I enjoy it as my form of exercise and relaxation."

"I didn't think those two words could be used in the same sentence."

Both women laughed before Penelope asked about Lindsay's leisurely pursuits.

"I have a membership at the Seattle Athletic Club. I prefer outdoor activities such as walking or biking, but it's nice to have a place inside to work out when the weather isn't so cooperative. And as you can see, I need all the help I can get." She swept her hand down the length of her body.

Lindsay was a full-figured woman, but certainly not what Penelope would consider fat or out of shape. "Nonsense, you're beautiful, Lindsay."

"Well, thank you for that, but as someone who's always been a bit larger than my peers, I've had some struggles. However," she said before Penelope could interrupt, as she was poised to do. "I've grown to love myself regardless of social views."

"Believe me, there's nothing to dislike about you. I can understand your struggles though. I've often been criticized for being too thin or unhealthy, and I love food!"

As both laughed, their lunches arrived. When they thanked the waitress, each began to enjoy their meals with conversation about one another.

Since much of Penelope's life was already public knowledge, there wasn't a great deal more that she could reveal to Lindsay. At the time of her mother's death due to a horrific car accident, stories ran rampant about the family and the world wondered about Bernard's future. Would he fall into despair, never to be heard from again? Would he marry another so that Penelope wouldn't be without a mother-figure?

What Bernard did was devote his attention to nurturing his daughter and his career, stating that he had had the love of his life and no one else could ever take her place. Of course it was much later in her life that Penelope learned this, given that she was barely two years of age at the time.

Even though she felt that she had experienced the feeling of love all those years ago with Sebastian, only to have it torn away, it paled in comparison to the love her father had expressed for his wife. But Penelope didn't want to divulge her past with Sebastian and how she now felt anxious at being reunited with him.

Penelope deflected the conversation away from herself, learning that Lindsay had been with the Symphony for two years now since graduating with her Master's in Music Theory from the University of Washington. When not involved with the orchestra she taught music part-time as well as volunteered with The Lullaby Project – a program where Symphony members worked with homeless mothers to write and record lullabies for their children.

"That must be very rewarding," Penelope said.

"It absolutely is," Lindsay answered. Her enthusiasm was palpable. "Growing up, music was always a part of our lives with my mom always singing to us. She had to make it fun to keep my older brothers engaged."

"Where is your family?"

"Eastern Washington."

"Do you get back home to visit often?" Penelope asked.

"Only around the holidays. My family has been over a few times for performances and to take advantage of seeing the Seahawks play at home. My brothers are football fanatics."

The two continued to enjoy their lunch as they talked about Seattle and the shopping they wanted to accomplish.

"You won't want in the area of shopping, that's for sure," Lindsay said. "From simple, everyday living at Target, to very upscale at Westlake Center and Pacific Place. Oh, and you'll have to experience Pike Place Market. It's amazing!"

Penelope was energized by Lindsay's continued enthusiasm. "I do need everyday items, and at least a pair of slacks and a blouse for tomorrow's dinner. Why don't we start at Target, and maybe Wednesday or Thursday we could do more at the other places you mentioned? I'll want something a bit more formal for Friday. Oh, and

I'll definitely need gowns for the performances."

"Looks like we're going to have lots of fun in the shopping department."

"Yes it does."

As they finished their lunches and Penelope paid, they made their way back out into the lobby.

"Thank you for lunch, Penelope, and for taking the time with me."

"Oh, Lindsay, it was my pleasure. I'm glad I'm making a friend."

"Me, too."

"Let me stop at the desk a moment. They have a shuttle service here and I want to make arrangements for a car to pick us up from our shopping. That way we won't have to carry all our purchases."

"Good thinking."

Penelope arranged for the car, also stating that they'd pick up Aria and take Lindsay back to her apartment before returning Penelope to the Fairmont. In the meantime, they took advantage of the day to walk the streets, allowing Penelope to become acquainted with the area and what it had to offer.

Once at their destination, they headed to the clothing section straight away. With Penelope finding a variety of items that she liked, Lindsay also convinced her to get a pair of skinny jeans, some funky tops, a sweatshirt, and a pair of athletic shoes.

"For your playful side." Lindsay winked at Penelope.

"I love these!" Penelope modeled the jeans and a sequined top while still wearing her flats.

Lindsay held out a new jacket for her to put on. "You look ready for a fun date. If I didn't have a class this evening, we could have so much fun at a club. I love dancing." Lindsay began taking the tags off of the clothes Penelope had on.

"Maybe another night," Penelope said as she gave her new friend a curious stare. "Um, Lindsay, what are you doing?"

"I'm taking the tags off so you can wear these right now. This outfit looks great on you, and well, since you're already in it, why change?" Lindsay smiled and shrugged. "You can take the tags and pay for them. Just fold up your own clothes and put them in the bag once you've made your purchases."

"Sure, why not?" Penelope grinned before retrieving her own

articles of clothing from the dressing room. They then made their way across the store for home items, toiletries, and groceries before heading toward the check-out.

"Got everything you think you need for now?"

"I think so. Thank you, Lindsay, this was fun."

"If you think this was fun, just wait until we start trying on gowns." She flashed a broad smile.

While Lindsay went through the line first, Penelope called the Fairmont for their ride. They left the store, found the car, and stowed their purchases away. Lindsay gave the driver directions to the groomer's in order to get Aria, then on to her apartment.

Penelope was delighted with Aria, and vice versa. Aria allowed Penelope to hold her while the driver helped Lindsay with her bags. Reluctantly, she released the cute little fluff ball into her mama's arms and said good night.

"I'll see you tomorrow at rehearsal."

"Yes you will. Have a good night," Lindsay replied.

Penelope turned to reenter the car as Lindsay slipped inside her apartment complex. She thanked the driver for his time as they returned to the Fairmont.

"You're welcome Ms. Dixon, any time."

As Penelope made her way up to her room, receiving help with her bags, her thoughts turned to the pool. She knew she'd never sleep if she didn't find a release for all the excitement that had built up from her afternoon excursion with Lindsay.

"Swimming would be perfect," she said to herself.

"Excuse me, Miss?" the attendant asked.

"Oh, just talking to myself. I'm thinking of heading down for a swim."

"It's a perfect time. Usually doesn't get much activity this time of day."

"It's settled then. A good swim and a light dinner to end the evening." She beamed.

"Yes, Miss." He returned her smile.

They arrived at her room, and once her bags were placed inside, she thanked the attendant.

"No problem at all. You have a good evening."

"Thank you. You as well."

Penelope closed and locked her door, then proceeded to change. She hated to take off her cute new outfit, but knew she'd have the opportunity to wear it again. Reflecting on the day as a whole, eager anticipation flowed through her at the new life she was paving for herself. She put on her swim suit, and over that she put on yoga pants and a loose top. Pulling on her sneakers, she grabbed her room card and headed out.

Chapter 6

Sebastian was restless.

As if stewing about the morning with Penelope and LaPelle, and wondering how he was going to make the coming weeks bearable wasn't enough to occupy his thoughts, he'd had a phone call earlier from Bernard Dixon to add to his turmoil.

"So how did your first day with Penelope go?"

"It went fine, Bernard. With the entire orchestra, in fact."

"And what did you think of my girl?"

Sebastian could hardly tell the truth on that one by divulging his long-time interest in his daughter. So he'd do the next best thing and only discuss what was relevant to their upcoming performances. "Penelope was magnificent. You should be very proud of her."

"Oh, I am. I admit that my decision to slow down and hers to go forth on her own, although inevitable, has been difficult for me. It's hard to fathom that my little girl is no longer that – my little girl."

"She's grown into a fine young lady. And her performance at rehearsal was wonderful. LaPelle was extremely pleased."

"I should hope so. Her drive and dedication are above reproach. Some may think I pushed my daughter in her musical studies, but truth is she pushed herself. She is a natural with a God-given talent that doesn't compare to most. Penelope always went at least two steps further than she needed to go, as if she had more to prove than anyone else."

"With you as her father, it's understandable."

"And I made it known that she had nothing to prove as my daughter. Whatever she chose to do, however she chose to do it, I'd be proud of her no matter what."

"You are an excellent father, Bernard."

"Hmm, I sometimes wonder. So often we look back and wish we'd done things differently. But I guess that's wasted energy." Bernard sighed.

"That can be said for anyone, Bernard, but the past is the past. We can only go forward from here." Sebastian had a feeling there had been more to his friend's statement that he didn't reveal, but thought if he had wanted to share, he certainly would have.

"Too true. Even though Penelope's talent would have been enough to secure the position with the Symphony, I couldn't resist pulling some strings to ensure that it happened."

"Ah, yes, about that. LaPelle let it slip that you might have had some influence in Penelope's position, to which she was understandably upset. She is very determined to prove herself without the help of others."

"Blast that man! I suppose I should be ready to receive a chastising call from her."

"On the contrary, I think he did a fine job of covering for you and telling Penelope that she would have had the position regardless. He's very taken with her."

"Well, now, that's excellent to hear. I shall thank him and still be ready to bow to my daughter. Now, about the collaboration. I just *knew* that you and Penelope would be great together. Your music is perfect for her. Hell, I should say she's perfect for your music." His boisterous laugh echoed through the line.

Bernard's mention of him and Penelope being great together sent a shiver of guilt through Sebastian. Best to set things straight right from the get-go. "Bernard, Penelope will do more than justice to any music, and I'm honored that she's debuting my piece, but this could very well be my last collaboration. I–"

"Nonsense! You're much too young to call it quits. You have so much more in you, I just know it."

"I didn't say I'd be calling it quits. I just meant that I may not be working with others after this. I prefer to do the composing and send my music out. To you, for instance."

"Did you miss the part where I said I was slowing down?" he

said, chuckling softly.

"I suppose it's just hard to fathom. You know how we old men are with change." In truth, Sebastian was beginning to question his desire all together. He felt as if he were at a crossroads and didn't know which direction to take.

"Old man, pah. There are still many more years of work in you. So you see, all the more reason for you to abandon this ridiculous notion. You and Penelope together would be–"

"Ah, Bernard, let's just take it one step at a time. Although I'm really looking forward to this series of performances, we'll see what decisions I make afterwards."

"Fair enough." After a brief pause, Bernard continued. "You know Sebastian, there's no one I trust more with Penelope than you."

And with that, the weight of the world seemed to settle on Sebastian's shoulders. He let the phone drop away as he closed his eyes and inhaled deeply before releasing a shuddering breath. How much longer could he bear the burden of his secret? When he returned the phone to his ear, he realized Bernard had continued speaking.

"-and look out for my girl."

"I'll do my best. I assume you'll be making it to Penelope's debut?"

"I wouldn't miss it. Now, I'll let you go so that you can enjoy your evening. You take care, Sebastian."

"You do the same, Bernard."

With that, Sebastian disconnected. Guilt and anguish rolled through him. He had to gain control of himself if he was to give justice not only to the Symphony, but to Penelope. The last thing she needed was more emotional confusion added to the pressures of her debut.

He promised himself that at the next opportunity, he'd make sure Penelope was clear on where they stood with one another. No matter how much it may kill him to once again deny his feelings for her, he still felt it best.

As his pent-up frustration continued to build, Sebastian knew he needed an outlet and decided a visit to the gym was in order. He changed his clothes and left his room, eager for the physical release.

Chapter 7

The pool was perfect. Penelope was alone, slicing through the water, working her muscles as hard as she could. Scissor kicks helped propel her as her arms plunged into the water, carving a path for her body. Every second stroke she turned her head to inhale, mindful of the approaching ledge. She already had her strokes counted and timed so that she knew when to prepare for her turn at the wall. Diving down, she somersaulted and kicked off from the pool's side, launching herself forward. As she broke through the surface, Penelope repeated the cycle.

Over and over she flew across the water. But for all the concentration she put into the activity, she was unable to quiet her thoughts on Sebastian and the dinner tomorrow evening. LaPelle was very eager for this interview and Penelope didn't want to disappoint. She reminded herself that this was a professional duty, nothing more.

Penelope made her last pass and decided to slow it down. As usual for her, she flipped onto her back intending to swim a few cool-down laps. She approached the wall and was ready to turn when a figure loomed above her. Pulling up short, she gasped and inadvertently took water into her mouth. Sputtering as she reached for the side of the pool, strong hands clasped hers and hauled her out of the water. Bringing her face to face with Sebastian.

What is he doing here?

Penelope's attempt at gaining composure was lost as she felt Sebastian's hands on her body, and their close proximity reminded her of his impressive form.

One of Sebastian's hands had slipped to her back and was rubbing soothing circles while the other cupped her chin, forcing her to look at his face. Worry lines marred his brow as his lips moved, but she couldn't hear a thing because of all the blood that rushed to her head. Her wet body was plastered against his, making her aware of the heat that radiated off of him as his muscles flexed with his every move.

Penelope's body betrayed her as gooseflesh broke out across her skin. She was chilled and heated all at once. Looking into Sebastian's eyes, her nipples contracted and her breath escaped on a near moan. And although he had stopped speaking, his lips didn't stop moving as they slowly lowered to brush with hers.

Tender at first, just a feather of a kiss, it may as well have been a mallet for all the force Penelope felt from it. Her legs threatened to give out on her, but Sebastian's arms held her tight against his solid form. The kiss deepened and she gave in to the dreamy feeling, matching his intensity and making it the most delicious kiss she'd ever experienced. Not that she had much to compare it to, given her limited encounters. It seemed like so long ago that Sebastian was her first kiss, and now, to be kissing him again…

She felt the bristle of his mustache and beard tickling her lips and skin. His heat threatened to melt her into a puddle of nothingness, and there was no mistaking the nudge she felt against her center as he pressed his hips closer to hers.

Sebastian broke away from her lips to trail kisses along her jaw and down her neck. She leaned her head back, closed her eyes, and called out to him.

"Bastian," she murmured, sighing in pleasure.

As if slapped, she felt him jerk away as he tried to untangle their entwined bodies. But Penelope held tight to his arms, preventing him from retreating as she looked into his eyes. She didn't want him to stop, and she certainly didn't want to see that look of regret all over his face.

"Don't," was all she said.

Sebastian halted his movements as his hands rested on her hips. "Penelope, I–"

"No, please don't say you're sorry. And please don't say that was a mistake, when it was the most wonderful thing I've ever experienced," she confessed.

She watched as his expression lit up in surprise while he looked down at her lips before returning his gaze to her eyes. "I'm not sorry, but it may have been a mistake. I–"

Penelope was quick to stop any further words from him as she pressed her lips back to his. She boldly ran her tongue across the seam, parting them, willing them to accept her invasion. And they did. Sebastian's mouth opened, allowing for her exploration. His hands tightened around her, pulling her in closer to once again feel his warmth; and his arousal.

Penelope nibbled and licked, testing herself as to how far she could go. *Would* go. Although they were alone, it was still a public space, and anyone at any time could enter. As soon as the thought entered her head, it faded just as quickly. She pressed on, mingling her tongue with his, delighting in the taste, the feel, even the sound as she realized they were both breathing heavily.

Penelope reached up to tangle her hands in his hair as she had wanted to do since first seeing him again. It felt soft and thick, and slightly damp. As she massaged his scalp, Sebastian ran his hands up and down her back, leaving a trail of heat that quickly dissipated in their absence.

The kiss became deeper, more urgent as Sebastian took over, thoroughly devouring her. He kissed across her cheek, stopping at her ear to lick. He sent chills across her entire body as he whispered her name. Slowly she released a long sigh, surrendering herself to his ministrations.

Penelope envisioned Sebastian scooping her up in his arms and whisking her away to his room. What a lovely fantasy that would be. But when he pulled back, she tried to protest. His words came before she could utter a sound.

"We need to stop before this becomes more than we can handle."

Penelope met his gaze with more boldness than she truly felt.

Act now before it's really too late.

"I can handle whatever you have to give me, Sebastian."

Sebastian closed his eyes, sighed, and pressed his forehead to hers. "I'm afraid it won't be enough."

"*You* are enough; that's all I need. It's all I ever needed," she said with near desperation in her voice.

Penelope watched the surprise on Sebastian's face as he leaned away from her. How could she make him see that her feelings had never diminished? Just seeing him again for the first time in years sent the passion she felt so many years ago flaring to life stronger than ever.

"No, Penelope, you needed more than I could give you. You *deserved* more."

"How can you say that?" She stepped back, causing his hands to fall away from her, and she hugged herself in a protective stance.

"Because it's true." His voice was filled with regret and sorrow. "You were so young; too young to really know what you wanted. I–"

"Don't tell me what I wanted and didn't want." She dropped her arms by her side, hands clenching into fists. "And don't tell me I was too young or that you were too old."

"I am ten years your senior! You were just a child at the time!" he said in obvious frustration, running his hands through his hair. "I couldn't take advantage of you; the daughter of my friend, practically my mentor."

"My father has nothing to do with this. He had nothing to do with my decision to love you!"

Another look of shock flashed across Sebastian's face before it quickly faded. "Oh, Penelope, you didn't love me." His face filled with sympathy as he shook his head. "We were infatuated with one another all those years ago, nothing more."

All Penelope felt now was disbelief and pain. Worse pain than when Sebastian had first rejected her. She couldn't believe he would so easily dismiss what was between them. And to have kissed her now the way he did, and imply that it was nothing? She felt ten times the fool for even thinking he may have still felt the attraction they'd once had. To think that he may have thought his decision in the past to refuse her was a mistake and maybe they could start anew.

And she had pressed on with the kiss, practically throwing herself at him. How mortifying!

Penelope was on the verge of tears, but she wouldn't let Sebastian see them. Backing up a few steps, she darted to the chair where her clothes lay and snatched them up. She wanted away from him; *now*. As he called her name and approached, she ran from the room, not giving him the chance to stop her.

Penelope bolted to the elevator, not caring about the trail of water she left in her wake. Frantically pushing the button, she willed the door to open before Sebastian reached her. If he even bothered to follow. Just as the door dinged, she jumped inside and pressed the button for her floor before stabbing at the button to quickly close the door. Before it shut, she saw Sebastian round the corner and make a sprint for her, calling her name. Thankfully the door shut before he made it, and the elevator began its upward journey.

Penelope collapsed against the wall, sinking to the floor. She let the tears flow freely as her emotions overwhelmed her.

What was I thinking? And how can I face him again?

She was relieved that the trip to the seventh floor was quick. Penelope wanted to get inside her room and shut out the world around her. Especially Sebastian.

—

Sebastian couldn't stop cursing himself for the loss of control. To think he was going to make sure she understood that there would be no emotional involvement between them. But seeing her beautiful body, holding her close and feeling her surrender to him pushed all those thoughts aside. To hear her declaration of love from all those years ago, and to think she may still love him… the hope was too much.

And what an idiot he had been to lie about his feelings and cause her such pain. Again.

After unsuccessfully making it to the elevator in time to stop her, he tore through the corridor to reach the stairs, taking them as fast as he could. He knew she was seven floors up. Bernard had informed him that Penelope was staying at the Fairmont, which had influenced his decision to stay there as well.

Now he was second-guessing his choice as he had done with so many of his decisions in the past.

Legs pumping, lungs burning, he reached Penelope's floor and flung open the door just in time to hear the elevator ding. He ran toward the sound, hoping he wasn't too late again.

As he came around a corner, Sebastian saw Penelope sliding her room card into its slot. Her head shot up at the sound of his approach and her eyes widened in panic. She wasn't having any luck with the door which gave him a few extra seconds to reach her before she slipped inside.

Sebastian managed a spurt of energy to sprint forward just as he heard the click of the lock and saw Penelope's hand grasp the handle. He made it to her door as she pushed it open, and he braced his hand on it to keep it from closing in his face.

"Penelope, let me–" his chest heaved as he tried to catch his breath.

"Go away, Sebastian." The strangled plea pulled at him as she tried to shove the door closed in his face.

He knew he had more strength than her and used it to his advantage. With more effort, he pushed into the room and cleared the door as it shut behind him. Watching Penelope back away from him, she had her clothes clutched tightly to her chest as if they were a shield with which she could protect herself. Sebastian hated seeing the look of fear mixed with despair on her face. She'd clearly been crying, her eyes swollen and red, her face pale; and still she was the most beautiful woman he'd ever seen. Knowing he'd caused her pain ripped at his heart. He somehow had to make things right.

"I'm sorry. The last thing in the world I wanted to do was hurt you."

She gave a cynical laugh as she said, "Well you failed miserably."

"I know, and I want to make it right." He continued to walk toward her slowly as she backed herself deeper into the room, bumping into a chair that was pulled away from the desk. She fumbled and dropped her shoes but kept backing up as if the thought of letting him get near her was frightening.

Well what did you expect after what happened at the pool, and now, forcing your way into her room?

"Penelope–"

"There's nothing you can do or say to make it right, so just leave. Please, Sebastian," she pleaded. "Leave me alone." She reached the edge of the bed and had no place else to run.

"I'm not leaving until you understand." He walked to within a few feet of her, wanting to touch her; comfort her.

"Oh, I understand. I understand that all those years ago you led me on and toyed with my emotions. Why? Because you were afraid? Cowardly? Or did you just enjoy stringing me along only to have your fill of an innocent young woman before bailing because it got to be too much?" Her face contorted with pain and confusion.

"No, I–"

"And now you're doing it again!" she interrupted, throwing her clothes on the floor. "I foolishly thought there might be some sliver of hope that you regretted your actions. That there may have still been a chance for us after all these years." She began to approach him now, a look of anger on her face, her blue eyes darkening with fire. "Never mind that you never once tried to contact me. And now we're adults, capable of making rational decisions. Capable of knowing what we want and being able to go after it. How stupid could I be?" she yelled, now standing within inches from him.

Sebastian watched as Penelope brought her arms up and shoved him. He stumbled back and did nothing to prevent her frustrations from unleashing. He deserved no less.

"I practically threw myself at you! Almost begged you not to stop, but to take me!" She ended with a strangled sob, shoving him again until his back hit the wall. Penelope's delicate hands fisted and began to pound on his chest as more sobs wracked her body. "I loved you, and now I've opened myself up to you again only to feel more heartache." Her tears flowed freely. Her hands clutched his shirt as her head fell forward, damp curls soaking the material.

Sebastian gently touched her arms. "Penelope." He had hoped to find the words to soothe her, but she flung her arms out, knocking his hands away. She backed away towards the bed again.

"Get out," she said quietly.

Sebastian took a step forward and watched her flinch as if she'd been struck. He instantly halted his movements. "Let me explain," he pleaded softly. He'd beg if he had to.

"No. I don't want your explanation," she said without emotion. "I want you to leave. *Now.*" She wrapped her arms around her shoulders, shrinking into herself.

He tried again, taking another step. "I–"

"Now!" She closed her eyes as more tears trickled down her face.

Sebastian sighed, unable to relieve the ache that settled in his hollow chest. Surely there was no heart in there any longer. How could there be after the depth of hurt he had caused her? He was torn between wanting to make her understand and following her demand. He'd be more of a selfish bastard if he stayed any longer, trying to convince her to see his side.

Sebastian looked at her once again as she stood frozen, eyes still closed. "You'll never know how truly sorry I am for your pain, Penelope," he said softly, hating that she once again flinched at the sound of his voice. He turned before she could respond; before she could open her eyes and reveal her pain.

Sebastian opened the door and exited. He stood outside until he heard the click of it closing. Feeling lower than he ever thought possible, he walked to the elevator and waited for the car to arrive. Once inside, he hit the button for his floor, only two levels down. Head resting against the wall, he wondered where the hell to go from here?

Chapter 8

As the door clicked shut, Penelope collapsed on her bed, curled into the fetal position, and let loose once again. Tears sprang forth and sobs shook her body until she ached. She didn't know how long she lay there, and she didn't care for that matter. Too tired to move, she grabbed the comforter to wrap around her, not bothering to crawl beneath the sheets. Asleep within minutes due to her exhaustion, she slept soundly without thoughts of Sebastian.

Later when Penelope woke, she realized the room was much darker. Pale light filtered in from the window by her bed. As she allowed her eyes to adjust, she slowly uncurled herself, feeling incredibly stiff and sore. A headache lingered, causing her to move cautiously. Coolness swept over her skin as she peeled off the blanket, also realizing that she had not taken the time to turn up the heat. Or more correctly, not had the *opportunity* to adjust the heat, given the encounter with Sebastian.

Just the thought of him brought a whimper from her mouth.

"No, don't go there right now," she said to herself, her throat raw and dry. She lifted herself off the bed and first went to kick up the heat, then checked her phone, seeing that it was nearly nine in the evening.

Wonderful. Good luck trying to sleep tonight.

After turning on the desk lamp, she went to the bathroom to shower. She stripped off her sticky swimsuit and dropped it on the floor. When the room began to steam from the hot water, Penelope stepped into the soothing spray. She stood beneath the comforting warmth and let the water pound on her neck and back. After a few minutes, she figured she'd better wash and rinse before her skin pruned.

Once she finished and turned off the water, Penelope grabbed one of the luxuriously thick towels and wrapped it around herself. She picked up her suit and other discarded clothes in the bedroom and placed them in a plastic bag for the laundry service. She then found some ibuprofen to take with a bottle of juice she'd purchased earlier. While drying, she thought about what to do with herself for the evening. It was too late to call her father or Lindsay, not wanting to disturb them, yet she wasn't tired enough to return to bed after having had that nap.

She scoffed at the idea that she'd taken a nap. She'd had a meltdown and needed to retreat from the world for a bit.

As her stomach growled, Penelope chuckled. "I want more than just some snacks," she said, thinking about what she bought earlier with Lindsay. She flipped through the directory of the hotel and found the dining section. Room service was an option, but she felt the need to get out of her room for a while. Seeing that one of the restaurants, Shuckers, was open for another hour and the attire was casual, she decided that that would be perfect.

Penelope pulled on her skinny jeans, tank top, and sweater, not bothering with a bra. She took the time to dry her hair with the diffuser attachment – just enough so that it didn't drip on her clothes or make her curls explode. After slipping on a pair of socks and her sneakers, she tucked her phone and room card into her pockets and headed out.

As Penelope entered the elevator, she tried not to relive what happened between her and Sebastian earlier, but her thoughts took her there anyway. She'd have to face him in the morning and be ever the professional. There was no way she would compromise her position with the Symphony and leave, just because of her past with the man. And she certainly wouldn't go running to LaPelle like some spoiled diva and request *not* to work with him. It was his piece after all, and she doubted Sebastian would turn tail and run either.

Or would he? He ran from her once...

Enough!

Penelope would deal with whatever came next and find the

strength to do what must be done.

Setting aside those thoughts, she exited the elevator and proceeded to the bar. She approached the entrance and was immediately greeted by a hostess.

"Good evening, do you have a reservation?"

"Oh, no, I don't," Penelope responded. "Do you have a table available?"

"How many in your party?"

"Just me."

The hostess smiled. "Follow me, please."

Penelope was led through the sparsely crowded room, noting several vacant tables. It was only Monday and well past dinner time. They stopped mid-way in and the hostess, whose name was Cheryl, indicated to a small table against the wall. "Will this do, Miss?"

"Yes, thank you, Cheryl. And it's Penelope."

Cheryl bowed her head. "Yes, I know. Penelope Dixon. Can I start you off with anything to drink? We have a full-service bar, along with a variety of sodas, sparkling water, juices, tea and coffee."

"Chamomile tea and water, no ice please." Penelope seated herself. "May I ask how you know of me?"

"Certainly. I follow the Seattle Symphony and read about you joining them. I'll leave our menu. Would you like to hear about our specials?"

"No, thank you though. I know what I'd like if I may order now?"

"Absolutely."

Penelope went on to order sautéed scallops with a Caesar salad. It would be a light enough meal for this late hour, yet still hold her until breakfast.

"We'll have that out shortly." Cheryl turned and walked away before Penelope could engage in any more talk.

"Thank you," she said, obviously more to herself. "Well she does have work to do," she mumbled.

A waitress returned with her water as Penelope pulled out her phone, opened up her email, and began reading through the itinerary for the Symphony. She was excited about the line-up for the performances, since she was familiar with the selections, and already knew Sebastian's piece by heart. She had to admit that his piece was extraordinary. Although unsure of how she'd react to his continued presence, she knew she'd do more than justice to his work.

Penelope read the details for Friday evening's party. LaPelle had informed the members that attire would not be formal, given the late notice, but to dress in business casual. *So a dress, skirt, or slacks would do*, she thought. She was glad to have found the outfits she did earlier, but was still excited about more shopping with Lindsay. Perhaps she'd find the perfect dress for Friday night.

She sighed, knowing that her schedule would move forward, regardless of her personal dilemma.

Penelope then opened the email detailing the dinner and interview she and Sebastian were to have tomorrow evening with Kimberly Beacham. They had reservations here in the Fairmont at The Georgian. She opened a link to read about Ms. Beacham and her work, impressed with what she found. No doubt it would be a terrific article and great advertisement for the Symphony and its schedule of performances.

She just had to find the strength to get through it and not allow her feelings about Sebastian intrude.

Before she could think more about what those feelings were, the waitress, whose nametag said Kiki, had returned with Penelope's dinner and tea.

"Is there anything else I may get for you?"

"No, thank you. This looks wonderful."

"Enjoy," Kiki said pleasantly before walking away.

Penelope efficiently finished her meal and drink, pondering what to do next. Returning to her room didn't sound appealing, and it was too late for her to take interest in exploring Seattle's nightlife – especially alone.

After signing for her dinner and charging it to her room, she strolled out to the lobby. Books and magazines were placed about on several of the tables, and a few people were taking advantage of the opportunity to relax and read. Penelope continued to meander, and eyed the piano on the second level that she'd noticed upon arrival. She walked up the steps and noticed the cover open, inviting her to take a seat at the bench. After striking a few keys, she immediately went into a rendition of Billie Holiday's "Foolin' Myself".

As Penelope played one song after another, she was unaware of the small crowd that had gathered below. All her choices were jazz, a favorite of hers that she didn't get to indulge in often enough. Before she realized it, she was playing "Cry me a River", and Cheryl, the bar hostess, surprised Penelope with her presence, joining in with the lyrics. Her voice was smooth and lovely, sounding very much like Julie London who had first recorded the song.

Cheryl had taken her dark blond hair down from its knot, allowing it to hang just past her shoulders. Her green eyes displayed the emotion that the song evoked. Penelope could just imagine her in a slinky cocktail dress rather than her crisp white shirt and black slacks.

When they were done, Penelope was once again surprised when applause broke out, obviously delighting the audience. She smiled at Cheryl who returned a brilliant one of her own.

"Your voice is beautiful," Penelope said to the approaching Cheryl.

"Thank you. And your playing is fabulous. Flawless. And all without any sheet music. No wonder you're with the Symphony."

Penelope chuckled. "I have a knack for picking up music rather easily."

"A child prodigy, like Emily Bear?"

Emily Bear was a well-known pianist/composer in the musical world whose talent was discovered at the young age of two. Although from Illinois, she quickly became known all over the world, making an unprecedented appearance on stage at Carnegie Hall at the age of nine. In her young life, she already had amazing accomplishments which included working with Quincy Jones who had produced one of her CDs. As if that wasn't spectacular enough, all the songs were original compositions of hers.

Penelope scoffed. "Hardly. That child is... well words can hardly describe. Besides, I've yet to try my hand at composing. Although I do adore jazz, as she does." Penelope chuckled. "I'd love for our paths to cross one day."

"Looks like music certainly agrees with you, as well as your admirers." Cheryl indicated to the crowd that had filled most of the chairs and sofas below.

Penelope stood and bowed to them, blushing and laughing. That brought about another round of applause. A soft voice called out "Encore".

"You're very humble about your talent."

Penelope turned to Cheryl. "Yes, well, I don't take for granted that I can make a living doing what I love. And how about you? You're either well trained or a natural talent. Do you perform publicly?"

"I do. I hostess here as well as perform with a group. Pays the bills, and to echo you, allows me to do what I love." Cheryl paused, looking out at the hotel lobby. She turned back to Penelope. "Shall we give them one more for the night?"

"Let's," Penelope agreed, grinning from ear to ear.

"Do you know, "The Nearness of You"?

Penelope nodded and returned to the seat. Cheryl started with the opening words before Penelope struck the keys once again. She watched Cheryl sing, performing the slow, sensual song with such grace, and was a little disappointed when the song came to an end with the last trailing notes.

More applause greeted them, and Penelope and Cheryl took a bow, laughing together.

"My shift ended at the bar, but would you care to have a drink with me?"

"I'd like that."

The two made their way down the stairs with Cheryl leading the way back to the bar. She asked the bartender, Rick, to set them up with two glasses of the House Riesling.

"Hope that sounds okay with you?" Cheryl asked.

"Perfect."

"So tell me about you, Penelope," Cheryl said with a smile.

"Not much to tell." Penelope shrugged. "You knew when I walked in who I was, yet you didn't let on."

"No, I didn't want to be presumptuous and address you as if I knew you, when we'd never been introduced before. Many stars like their anonymity, and you looked like you wanted to be plain ol' Penelope tonight. Not international star pianist."

"Well, thank you for that, although I'd hardly call myself a star," she scoffed.

"Oh, I'd say you are. The symphony posting had a very nice story about you and your father."

Before Penelope responded, Rick set a glass of wine in front of her and she thanked him. He returned with, "You're welcome" and a flirty wink.

"I hadn't got around to reading it. I don't usually read the promotions or reviews."

"Really? And why is that?" Cheryl sipped her wine as she studied Penelope.

Penelope shrugged as she also sipped her wine, enjoying the sweet taste. "I suppose it doesn't really matter what is said or written, I'm going to perform the same no matter what."

"Smart attitude. So, can I jump right in and ask about your broken heart?"

Penelope was taken aback by Cheryl's question. "How do you know I have a broken heart?" This time she took a healthier sip of her wine.

"I'm pretty good at reading people. Also, I could tell from your choice of songs earlier. You seemed to touch on sad love songs. But then, many jazz songs do, don't they?" She chuckled at the realization. "And you didn't even blush at our flirty Rick, who manages to charm every female who walks through that archway." She nodded to the bar's entrance.

Penelope laughed lightly before mumbling about having enough of men for some time. When she received a questioning look from Cheryl, she didn't feel like elaborating, so she asked Cheryl about herself.

"Nice deflection," Cheryl quipped, to which Penelope just shrugged again, looking almost smug.

"Well, I've been singing since childhood, watching my mom dance and sing around the house. I remember watching "The Fabulous Baker Boys" with her, and Michelle Pfeiffer singing "Makin Whoopie". I thought, *wow*! Not that I wanted to slide around on top of a piano, mind you," Cheryl added with a low chuckle. "I wanted to sing, so I started performing at clubs and got the attention of some others who wanted me to join their group. And I did." Cheryl took another drink before continuing. "That was eight years ago, and we've done a decent job of getting recognition in the Northwest."

"So you travel for performances? What about your job here?"

"That's the nice thing about my job here; there are two others who hostess as well, each of us having other jobs or commitments in our lives. And yes, I travel at least once a month for shows, as well as perform at least weekly in the Seattle area."

"What's the name of your band and where's your next performance?"

"Our group is called Euphoria, and we play this weekend at The Triple Door Lounge. It's just behind Benaroya Hall on Union. You should come down. We play Friday and Saturday, at nine."

"I'd like that, thank you."

"You're welcome. Now, back to the subject of heartbreak. Anything you care to get off your chest? I'm well versed on the subject."

"Is that so?" Penelope laughed. "Had your share of it as well?"

"Hasn't every woman at least once in their lives?"

"This is my second time around, only with the same man ten years apart." And with that, Penelope swallowed the last of her wine. Rick appeared in an instant, offering to refill her glass. Penelope politely declined, to which he gave an exaggerated pout and presented a glass of water.

"Men," Cheryl teased as she waved Rick away, causing Penelope to laugh. She then turned back to Penelope. "That can't be easy."

"No, it isn't. And I told myself I'd not think of it the rest of the night. Tomorrow will come soon enough to face him again."

"He's with the Symphony then?"

"Not really. He's a composer that's collaborating for our upcoming performances."

"No shit? Sebastian Mauer?" Cheryl quickly apologized for that comment when Penelope choked on her water.

"So you know of Sebastian?"

"I follow the symphony, remember? And I read the announcement of his collaboration."

"I guess if I'd read through all the emails Maestro had sent me prior to coming here, I'd have been more prepared to face him."

"Anything I can help you with?" Cheryl continued to nurse her wine while watching Penelope.

"Not unless you can tell me how to fall *out* of love with him?" She nearly pleaded as she gave Cheryl a hopeful expression.

"That, I'm afraid, I can't help with. I know firsthand about loving someone you wished you wouldn't. Time and distance helps; somewhat."

Penelope's expression deflated. "Evidently not in my case. After all this time apart, one look had me ready to shamelessly throw myself at him."

"You didn't?" Cheryl snorted.

"Well, no, not when I first saw him. That would have been embarrassing in front of the entire orchestra and director LaPelle. But earlier this evening, he surprised me at the pool. And, well, let's just say he made it clear that we can never be."

"I'm sorry, Penelope."

"Thank you, Cheryl. I can't believe I'm opening up to you like this. I didn't mean to dump my problems on you."

"You're not. I asked, remember?"

"So what happened to *your* love interest?" Penelope inquired.

"I left him back in Chicago."

"Really? How long ago was that?"

"I traveled back there with Euphoria for Chicago's Annual Jazz Festival, not quite three years ago. We caught the attention of some influential people and were invited to perform. They hold it every year right before Labor Day. Well, long-story-short, I met Toby and it was love at first sight. Or so I thought. More like lust at first sight," she snorted. "After a blistering week together, he told me what we had was fun, but he disappeared and I never heard from him again. After I returned home to Seattle, I nursed a broken heart for a while, but then decided to get on with my life."

"Just like that?" Penelope asked skeptically.

"Hardly. I went through a bad period, depression, hooking up with lots of guys for one-night-stands. It wasn't pretty, or healthy. Thankfully, my band mates helped me get my act together. No pun intended." She smiled, but there was a hint of sadness to it.

"Have you had a serious interest since Toby?" Penelope noticed that Cheryl sipped her wine, making the one glass last.

"Nah. And it's not because I'm holding out hope that one day he'll return and sweep me off my feet. I learned there are no fairy tale endings in my future. No, I poured myself into my music and my friends. I'm still not ready to date one-on-one; I group date instead."

"Group date?"

"Yeah, it's just a bunch of friends who get together for dinner and fun, no expectation of anything other than enjoying each other's company. And at the end of the night, we all go our separate ways."

"That does sound fun, without the worry or drama."

"Exactly!" Cheryl lifted her wine glass, offering to toast with Penelope.

Penelope lifted her glass and gently knocked it against Cheryl's.

"So, about facing Sebastian tomorrow," Cheryl started. "Since you can't distance yourself from him, the way I see it, there are only two ways to deal with the situation. One, if you really love him and feel he's worth it, you face him and give an ultimatum. Tell him exactly that – that the love you two have is worth a shot, and if he realizes what an idiot he was and throws himself at your mercy, then you've got him."

"And number two?"

"If you tell yourself right now that you don't see him changing his mind, then you pull yourself up and say it's his loss. You go on like the strong woman I think is lurking in there." Cheryl raised her finger to point at Penelope's chest.

"You make it sound so easy," Penelope said.

"Believe me," Cheryl said, patting Penelope's shoulder. "It's anything but easy. But you can't sit in limbo, waiting on something to happen. You have to make it happen; whatever that *it* may be. Only *you* can live your life, Penelope."

Penelope reached up to cover Cheryl's hand with hers. "Thank you. That's probably the best thing anyone's said to me in a long time."

"Really? What kind of people have you been hanging out with?" she teased as she withdrew her hand.

"No one else that I've confided in about Sebastian, so thank you again."

"You're welcome." Cheryl slid her glass away and Rick appeared in front of her. "Thanks, Rick, these are on me."

"Oh, let me," Penelope said.

"No, no, my treat. You can repay me by coming by to see us this weekend."

"I definitely will. I have another engagement early Friday evening, but maybe afterwards."

"Need any company?" Rick slyly interjected with a devilish grin. He cleared the glasses and wiped down the bar while lingering in front of Penelope.

And while Penelope could appreciate his cuteness, she wasn't anywhere near ready to move on to another man. One was enough to deal with right now, and she had to figure out just how to go about that by morning. "Um…"

"Stop flirting, Rick," Cheryl said. "This one's off limits."

"Too bad." And with that he shot another wink to Penelope before he walked away.

"He does that with all the pretty ladies," Cheryl said. "Not that you aren't worthy of pursuit," she quickly added.

Penelope laughed. "It's all right. The last thing I need is another man to muddle my brain." After slipping off the stool, Penelope thanked Cheryl again for the drink and company.

"My pleasure. I look forward to seeing you again."

They said their good byes and parted ways. Cheryl walked to the back of the bar while Penelope made her way out to the elevator. It was eleven and still Penelope wasn't ready for sleep. She thought she'd go back to her room and maybe do some reading before trying to get more rest.

She was going to need it for what lay ahead.

Chapter 9

Tuesday morning dawned with a steady drizzle of rain as grey skies blanketed the city. Penelope stood in her robe peering out her window as she drank coffee, trying to infuse her chilled body with its warmth. She also needed its kick of caffeine to get her going after the restless night she'd had.

Turning away from the window, she moved to the closet to choose her outfit for the day. She slipped off the robe and into a pair of leggings, then added a tank, a sweater dress, and knee-high socks. Her well-worn sable riding boots were next, as they would protect her feet much better than her flats, and add more warmth for her legs.

After finishing her coffee, Penelope added cream to her hair to tame the curls that were sure to go crazy in the humidity. She collected her satchel and her phone before grabbing her coat and heading out the door.

Penelope still hadn't come to any conclusion on how to deal with Sebastian. Her first notion was to act as if the scene at the pool had never happened, and pray that he would do the same. But the chances of that happening weren't very likely. Sebastian seemed determined to make Penelope understand his decision and reasoning behind it. She didn't think he'd push the issue in front of the entire symphony, but no doubt he'd try to persuade her to take a moment alone with him.

That, she had to ensure, would not happen.

During the elevator ride down, Penelope tried to make sense of her true feelings for Sebastian. Were they only the result of a young girl's infatuation? Had she held on to a dream all these years only to realize it was wasted time? It was obvious there was something between them, and even if he didn't want to admit it, Sebastian felt it too. But why would he deny it?

Was it even worth exploring?

She thought of what Cheryl had advised; facing him head on or putting him in the past in order to move on. Neither decision appealed to her right at the moment, so she decided to give herself more time to consider every variable.

"Why, so you can further torture yourself?" she murmured under her breath.

Penelope tried to put her thoughts elsewhere; like another shopping excursion with Lindsay. She'd also be sure to invite Lindsay to accompany her to see Cheryl and her band this weekend, if she didn't have plans of her own.

Once the elevator stopped, Penelope stepped out and collided with the man who continued to invade her thoughts.

"I'm sorry, Penelope," Sebastian said, grabbing ahold of her arms. "This wasn't how I had planned to say good morning," he quipped.

Penelope quickly retreated so that Sebastian's hands fell away. "I'm all right."

"Are you?" he asked softly. As if he truly cared.

Penelope's head snapped up to face him, determined to show strength instead of the weakness she had shown last night. "Yes, Sebastian, I'm fine. Now, if you'll excuse me." She turned toward the exit, hoping to put distance between the two of them. Fruitless, she knew, since he was headed in the same direction as her.

"May I walk with you to the Hall?" he called out as she passed the concierge.

"You're free to walk wherever you want." Her answer was clipped. She quickened her strides, thankful that the rain had lessened and she wasn't at risk of slipping and making a fool of herself. Pedestrian traffic was fairly light, allowing Sebastian to easily catch up to her.

His voice reached out to her. "I can understand you wanting to keep your distance, but I hope that you're still willing to continue working together."

She nearly came to a stop in order to face him, almost insulted that he'd think she'd reconsider. After her brief hesitation, she pushed on, ready to get to rehearsal. Ready to be surrounded by others instead of being pursued by Sebastian. "Of course I want to continue with the collaboration," she called out. "It's not like I could call a halt to it anyway. This is important for the Symphony. And it's important to me."

"Thank you for that, Penelope."

His voice reached out to her, sounding sincere, and Penelope wanted to groan as her insides weakened just a fraction. She was just about to cross University when she felt a tug on her arm. Her backside collided with Sebastian's front as a bicyclist whizzed by, clipping her satchel but thankfully doing no damage.

"Are you okay?" Sebastian whispered in her ear.

All Penelope could do was nod as she took a moment to get her heartrate under control. She didn't know if it raced more because of the near collision with the cyclist, or the fact that she was pressed against Sebastian's hard body. His hands remained on her arms, his heat burning into her, and she found her head leaning back against him.

When she realized what she was doing and Sebastian's hands slid up to her shoulders, she quickly stepped away.

"Thank you," Penelope said softly. "I'm usually not so inattentive."

Sebastian slid his hands into the pockets of his coat. "Yes, well, I'm sure you've got a lot on your mind. Like escaping from me." He almost looked ashamed.

"I- I'm not trying to escape from you," she stuttered. "I just don't want to be late for rehearsal." Penelope felt her face flush, knowing he wasn't far from the truth. As much as she longed to be near him, it hurt too much.

"Penelope, I'm sorry. I need you to understand that I never meant–"

"Not now, Sebastian. Not here." She turned away from him, and after scanning both ways, hurried across the street and on to Benaroya Hall. Penelope practically sprinted to the entrance, bypassed Starbucks, and skipped out on her favorite Frappuccino in order to be amongst the others. She flung open the door to the recital hall and sought out Lindsay who was thankfully already in her chair, looking her way.

As Penelope approached her new friend, she heard the door open behind her and assumed it must be Sebastian who followed. She didn't dare look to confirm, instead called out to Lindsay.

"Hi, Penelope," Lindsay greeted in response. "How are you this morning?"

"Just fine, thank you. Before we get started and I forget to ask, do you have plans Friday evening after the reception at Tulio's?"

"No, I don't. What do you have in mind?"

"Well, I wondered if you'd like to go to The Triple Door Lounge? I know of the group that'll be performing there." Just as she finished, she noticed Sebastian nearby speaking with another member of the orchestra, and she couldn't help but look that way. He lifted his head and their gazes held one another's before Penelope looked away, giving her attention back to Lindsay.

"Oh, I'd really like that. One of our saxophonists has played there before and it's a great venue."

Penelope smiled and nodded at Lindsay. "Great!"

"So, did you get that swim in like you wanted yesterday?"

The mention of her swim brought back flashes of her encounter with Sebastian; bringing heat to her cheeks and causing a dull ache in her chest. *Will I ever be able to control these reactions?*

"Uh, yes, I did get to swim. I, uh, still had a restless night. But I met Cheryl," she quickly added before Lindsay could question her further. "She's a hostess at the Fairmont's Shuckers Bar, and she sings. It'll be her and her band, Euphoria, playing at the Triple Door Lounge Friday."

"Sounds good. I'll look forward to that. Are you ready for your interview tonight?"

"I suppose so." She shrugged, trying to show indifference. "I'll just be answering questions about the Symphony and our performances."

"Don't be surprised when personal questions come up. They always do." Lindsay had assembled her flute and placed her sheet music on her stand.

"That's fine," Penelope answered. "There's not much to tell in that department."

"Uh, huh," Lindsay looked at Penelope and lowered her voice. "Are you sure about that? Because the way Mr. Sebastian Mauer is emitting those possessive vibes, it's a wonder there isn't a gilded cage around you, locked down tight."

All Penelope could do was stare open-mouthed at Lindsay, stunned by her comment.

"And don't look at me like I don't know what I'm talking about. Not after seeing your intense encounter with him yesterday after rehearsal. And now, you practically came running in here as if someone were throwing fireworks at your heels, and who should follow you? None other than the handsome composer himself. Penelope, are you okay?" Lindsay stood and set her flute on her chair before she walked around her stand, coming to Penelope's side.

"Not really," Penelope confessed. She felt the weight of her secret and couldn't bear it any longer. She thought she could be stronger, more mature; but she felt incapable of handling this on her own. *How pathetic is that, that I want my independence, yet at the first hurdle, I stumble?*

Then she felt Lindsay's hand on her arm. "Come with me," she said gently.

Penelope was led out of the room and down the hall to the restroom. Rehearsal was about to start at any moment, but she didn't really care about that just now. She needed to clear her head in order to focus on moving forward.

Lindsay led them both to a sitting couch in the foyer of the restroom. "What's going on?"

"I'm in love with Sebastian," she admitted quickly, instantly feeling relieved. "I have been for ten years."

Lindsay's eyebrows shot up and her mouth opened, ready to say something. She then relaxed her look as she stared at Penelope, giving her sympathy. Finally, she said, "There's more to this story. You two obviously aren't together now as a couple, are you?"

"No. I was seventeen when we met, months away from my eighteenth birthday. My father and I were performing in Vienna. Sebastian was there as well for their New Year's Concert. It was a great honor to be asked to perform. The grandeur was all very exciting. That was when my father and Sebastian really struck up their friendship, greatly admiring each other's work, which led to their future endeavors."

Penelope went on, detailing the moment they were introduced, and the magical evening that followed. "It was truly like a fairy tale. He was the most handsome man I'd ever met. So reserved, courteous, and attentive. So smart and humble. He later told me that he felt as if he'd been struck by Cupid." Penelope scoffed. "After our performances, we spent the evening together at a gala. We danced and talked and had the most wonderful night. And although we already rang in the New Year, Sebastian and I shared a kiss that was amazing. I was so swept up in him, it was unbelievable."

"Wow, after only one evening together? What did your father think?"

Penelope wrung her hands together nervously, her heart racing just reliving the joy of the time she and Sebastian had shared, and the secret they had kept from her father.

"He didn't attend the gala and had been unaware. At least I never came out and told Father of my attraction to Sebastian. He had been the first man I'd ever had that kind of reaction to, and I had been equally afraid of it as I'd been overjoyed. I knew Sebastian had reservations about our age difference, but I never realized just how much that seemed to come between us until recently. I still don't know the true reason why Sebastian ended what we had.

"After two days in Vienna, Father and I returned home, and I knew Sebastian was off to Australia for a performance before heading back to the States. We spoke often and exchanged emails. When he returned, he came to San Francisco for a visit and spoke with my father about transitioning into composing. We managed to find time to spend together, and I knew I was hopelessly in love with him. I could just imagine our future together, in music, in marriage. I replayed the whole fantasy over and over in my mind countless times."

"And your father never had a clue? How is that possible?"

"Well, Sebastian and I always met in secret. It added to the excitement of us being together. If Father did suspect us, he certainly didn't confront me about it. I can't imagine him not speaking to me about it if he knew. I honestly don't know if he would have been happy or upset. He treasured the friendship that he and Sebastian developed, and I know he would have wanted us both to be happy."

"And Sebastian ended it between you two?" Lindsay asked.

"Yes, after nearly six months. During that time I had turned eighteen, an adult in the eyes of the law. Most people considered me an adult by the time I was a teen."

"You do have a very mature quality about yourself."

Penelope laughed, although it was strangled. "Right now I feel anything but mature. I'm trying so hard to prove I can be an independent woman who can make it on her own, but I'm at a loss as to how I should handle Sebastian. A few months after my eighteenth birthday, he suddenly said that our relationship could no longer be." Her voice hitched as if stuck in her throat. "He and my father continued their collaborations via long distance, which over time began to lessen. Sebastian never paid another visit to our home again, and Father never questioned Sebastian's sudden earnest in staying away from touring and the media. We never crossed paths again."

"Until yesterday," Lindsay cut in.

"Yes." Penelope nodded.

"Did your father never notice changes in you? How could he not see that his daughter was in love and then in pain?"

"As much as my father and I love one another, we are very reserved about discussing or showing our emotions. I never told him about my love for Sebastian, and I hid my heartache well. I went away for a short period of time after Sebastian broke it off, so I had an opportunity to get over the worst of it without my father knowing. I spent three months in New England visiting with family from my mother's side. I used the excuse that I wanted to build a stronger relationship with them, as I didn't see them nearly as often as I would have liked."

Lindsay grabbed Penelope's hands and held tight. "Oh, Penelope. You had no one to help you through that. And then to come face to face with him again and have your world thrown off-kilter. You seemed so calm yesterday."

"Hardly. I was a mess. I just found a way to hide it. Well, that is until now."

"Something happened, didn't it?"

Penelope closed her eyes and nodded. When she opened her eyes again to see Lindsay's continued look of sympathy, she almost sobbed. Realizing strength was what she needed, she was determined to fine it; and part of being strong meant asking for help. "Yesterday, Sebastian was at the pool, and, well, we had an encounter."

"An encounter? You fought, you made up? What?"

"We kissed. I practically threw myself at him, told him not to say that what we had had been a mistake." Penelope stood up abruptly, breaking contact with Lindsay. She felt the need to move, so she paced a few steps before turning back to do it again.

"And how did he respond?" Lindsay asked.

Penelope looked to Lindsay who was watching her intently. "Oh, he responded. He kissed me like his life depended on it, but then said that it *was* a mistake. He tried to explain why, but I wouldn't let him. I felt so humiliated. Again. How could he respond that way? How could he kiss me like I was the air he needed to breathe, only to deny it?" Penelope threw her hands up in frustration.

"I don't know," Lindsay said softly. "You still love him."

Penelope plopped back down on the couch and stared at the ceiling. "Yes. All these years later, and yes, I still love him. How pathetic is that?"

"No, it's not," Lindsay answered with tenderness. "But you need to figure out if he still loves you, and if that love is worth pursuing."

"That's exactly what Cheryl said last night. She said I either confront him or move on. It *sounds* simple, although it certainly doesn't feel that way." Penelope turned her face towards Lindsay. "I was devastated years ago; I don't know if I can go through that again."

"Penelope, I'm not going to blow smoke up your backside and say that it'll be easy, or that you can move on, or whatever. It obviously hasn't been easy. And to say that you're young and you'll find love again if it isn't with Sebastian, well, that's just insulting. While I've never been in your situation, I can sympathize with your emotions.

"But you can't go on in limbo. You have to face this man every day for the next three weeks. In order to do that, you need to know where you stand with one another." Lindsay took Penelope's hands again. "You control your life, Penelope. No one else."

Penelope pulled Lindsay in for a hug. She wasn't normally a demonstrative person, but at the moment she needed the contact, the comfort. She needed to feel grounded. "Thank you," she whispered, feeling Lindsay's nod.

A loud bang at the door startled both women, and when they looked up, a custodian was entering with her cart. "Oh, pardon me, ladies. I was told there was a concern here, but I can come back later."

"No, no, that's quite all right," Penelope said hurriedly as she and Lindsay released one another and stood. "We really should be getting back to rehearsal."

"I'm surprised LaPelle isn't bellowing about our whereabouts." Lindsay snickered as they made their way toward the door.

"You ladies have a good one." The custodian called out as she pushed her cart to the end of the room.

Penelope and Lindsay made their way back into the recital hall and noticed that their director had yet to appear. They grinned at one another before moving toward their seats, only to notice that many of the members were packing their instruments away. Before Penelope could question what was happening, she watched Sebastian make his way toward her. She fought the urge to turn away. Instead, she faced him, drawing on the strength that Lindsay and Cheryl felt she possessed.

Time to find out.

Chapter 10

"Penelope, are you okay?" Sebastian asked when he reached her side.

"I'm fine," she said abruptly. "What's going on? Why are they packing up?" She indicated to the other musicians. "And where is LaPelle?"

"While you were out, an administrator came in to notify us that he wasn't going to be in today, that he was suddenly ill. I guess it was more than just allergies affecting him. So, there's no conductor."

"So no practice?" When she saw Sebastian shake his head, she pursed her lips. "Well that's silly. We have the music. You can conduct today," she heard herself say. She wasn't surprised to see Sebastian's stunned expression. "There's no sense in wasting time. We're all together, so we might as well make the most of it. Besides, who knows how long LaPelle will be out?" Before she gave Sebastian a chance to respond, she was clapping her hands in order to gain the attention of the other members.

"Excuse me," she said, barely raising her voice. When only a few gave her their attention, she tried again. She inserted her fingers in her mouth and produced a shrill whistle. That most definitely got everyone's attention. Penelope turned to Lindsay and gave her a wink. In return, she got a thumbs-up. "I realize LaPelle is out sick, but let's not waste what precious time we have together. Sebastian is fully capable of leading us in today's rehearsal. So please, everyone take your seats and we'll begin."

Many of the members of the orchestra shared questioning looks with one another, waiting to see who was going to comply. When most returned to their seats, murmuring in agreement, everyone else followed suit.

Penelope sat at the piano and proceeded to take out her music and place it above the keys – not that she really needed it. Knowing that Sebastian was right at her side, probably ready to rebut her assumption of him leading the group, she turned to him and flashed the best smile she could. "Ready when you are, Maestro." She knew her words must have sounded like a challenge… perhaps that's what she had meant all along.

Sebastian kept his gaze on her, not saying a word. Just when she thought he would decide to refuse, he gave her a nod and turned. Feeling victorious – as well as relieved – Penelope grinned and had to stifle a giggle. She cleared her throat as she watched Sebastian take his place behind the conductor's podium.

As Sebastian stood there, a member of the orchestra approached him with her booklet of music. She placed the sheets before Sebastian as she spoke softly with him. After a moment, she returned to her seat amongst the violinists.

"Maggie has been kind enough to share with me the music that we'll be rehearsing." Sebastian nodded in her direction. "Thank you all for remaining, and trusting me to lead you. Let's begin."

Their first piece was Tchaikovsky's Piano Concerto No. 1, which began with a flourish, and Penelope was all too ready to perform.

Piece after piece, Sebastian led the symphony beautifully through four compositions. Occasionally, Penelope had the opportunity to watch him, and she could have easily spent the day doing just that. His composure and skill were impressive. His passion and mannerisms were stunning and powerfully sexy.

Penelope pulled her thoughts away from that line of thinking, knowing they were futile. She had to focus on her performance and her professionalism; putting her personal feelings and longings in the back of her mind. She'd deal with Sebastian and the situation later.

They played non-stop, saving Sebastian's piece as the fifth and final one. And once again, the performance was masterful. The entire orchestra gave Sebastian a standing ovation, to which he bowed and clapped, congratulating them on a magnificent rehearsal.

"I'll try to ascertain LaPelle's condition and report to everyone this evening. If he's still unavailable, we'll see how that will affect the coming days."

"I'd say you were a perfect replacement," Henry offered. "I would support you leading us until LaPelle is able to return. That is if you agree to it." Many others voiced their support.

"Thank you for that," Sebastian said humbly. "Let's still plan on our regular schedule of rehearsal at 9 AM tomorrow, and look for my email this evening."

As many called out their good byes and good nights, Penelope closed the lid over the keys and gathered her music. When she looked up, Lindsay and Sebastian were headed her way, both calling out to her. Once in front of her, Sebastian spoke first.

"I don't mean to interrupt your plans, Penelope, but would you spare me a moment before you leave? It's about this evening's interview."

"Certainly," she answered. She looked from Sebastian to Lindsay then back to Sebastian again after seeing Lindsay's questioning grin.

"Thank you." He turned to Lindsay and said good evening before he retreated toward the exit.

Lindsay then spoke, asking if Penelope would be okay.

"Yes, I'll be fine. He's not the big, bad wolf."

"Are you sure? Because the look he gave you said he would be ready to eat you up." She looked at her watch and grinned. "It is lunch time, after all."

"Lindsay!" Penelope couldn't help but laugh as Lindsay did too.

"What? Tell me you wouldn't let him?"

"You're not helping my cause." Penelope gave her a gentle hip check while continuing to giggle.

"Maybe I am, maybe I'm not. But I like seeing you laugh rather than cry." She slipped her arm around Penelope's shoulders and gave her a squeeze before stepping back.

"Thank you. I'd prefer to laugh as well." Penelope lifted her coat and satchel as Lindsay shifted her belongings in her arms.

"Call me later and tell me how dinner goes." Lindsay winked.

"You do realize that it's an interview, not a romantic dinner," she said, slinging her satchel across her body and folding her coat across her arm.

"It can be both."

They walked toward the exit, snickering like little girls. "I'd prefer it remain business–" Penelope started when Lindsay interrupted.

"Until it doesn't. There's definitely something there between you two, and I'm rooting for ya."

"Thanks. I guess?"

"You'll be fine," Lindsay said as they reached the door. Once they walked through, both women saw Sebastian waiting across the foyer. "Good luck." She then wished Penelope a good night.

I'll need that and more.

—

Sebastian had barely been able to leave the recital hall without visibly shaking as adrenaline coursed through body, his heart ready to pound out of his chest. Standing in front of the Symphony, leading the rehearsal had been an exhilarating rush he hadn't anticipated. When Penelope had first suggested it – or rather, commanded it – he'd been on the verge of refusing. Yes, he had been a performer and a composer, but he'd never led an orchestra. Turns out, it wasn't difficult for him at all. He had actually enjoyed it. But could he continue to do it if LaPelle were to be out more days? Sebastian believed he could, but the question remained, would he be allowed to? Or would the higher-ups find another replacement if it came to that?

He purchased a bottle of water to quench his dry mouth as his thoughts ruminated.

Penelope seemed to have recovered from their encounter last night, proving her strength and maturity. Or did it mean that she had just that quickly decided Sebastian had been right and that they shouldn't pursue a personal involvement?

But *had* he been right? Could they try again? Would it be possible to mend the hurt and work on a relationship? Could they –

"Sebastian?"

Penelope's soft greeting brought him out of his thoughts. He spun to face her, still in awe of her beauty and the effect it had on him. Her presence alone seemed to empower him; allowing him to face anything that came his way.

Why did I push her away? And could I ever make it up to her and be worthy of her love again?

The thought struck him so suddenly, his heart raced even faster. His vision tunneled, and at the end of it, the only thing he could focus on was her. His Penelope. The urge to rush to her and envelop her in his arms was overwhelming. All he could do was act, consequences be damned.

Sebastian's stride had him in front of her in a heartbeat. He took her hand and practically pulled her around a corner and into an alcove, tossing his bottle of water in a receptacle on the way. With his adrenaline surging again, stronger than when he had just led the symphony, he didn't try to analyze his actions. He went where his emotions led him. Where his desire begged him to go.

"Sebastian, what are you doing?"

He didn't bother with an explanation, easily pulling her with him, as she was probably too stunned to protest. Not that it would've helped her. Sebastian was on a mission – to conquer this woman.

Once out of sight of anyone else, Sebastian gently pressed her against the wall, his body trapping her, one hand still holding hers, the other cupping her cheek. Her startled expression excited him; her brilliant blue eyes questioned his intentions.

They stood silent, assessing one another. Just as Penelope's mouth parted to speak, Sebastian captured her lips with his. He meant to start gently, but the contact took his breath away; along with all rational thoughts. Her sweet taste only made him crave more. And more, he took. His hand slid up, tangling in her hair, cupping the back of her head. He parted his lips, allowing his tongue to sweep across her seam, begging for entrance into her mouth.

Surprisingly she opened for him, and he didn't give her a second to rethink. Sebastian dove in with a force that had them both moaning, both pressing harder against one another. Their tongues swirled, their lips clashed. He felt her pull her hand from his, her other dropping her coat as she sunk both hands into his hair, pulling him in closer. *As if I'd try to pull away.* Her taste was intoxicating, her touch electrifying. Sebastian couldn't get enough.

He brought his free hand around her back, pulling her in tight. Penelope gasped into his mouth as he ground their bodies together, his arousal leaving no doubt as to the effect she had on him. And still it wasn't enough. He couldn't get close enough; he couldn't touch and taste her enough.

"God, I want you," Sebastian rasped as his lips left her mouth to suckle at her ear.

"Yes." Her response escaped on a breath as her hands raked his scalp.

Sebastian continued his assault, his lips peppering kisses along her jaw as his hands moved down to her dainty little rear. He voiced his frustration in a growl when the high collar of her dress prevented him from exploring more of her tantalizing flesh. He latched on to her lips once again with urgency as he squeezed her bottom. Penelope squealed, delighting him.

He broke contact to look at her face. Bringing his hands around, he retreated a fraction to skim up her abdomen and brush her breasts, watching her body respond to his touch. Eyes closed, she sighed and moved with his hands as if she were his marionette; his to control.

And he wanted to control her.

He wanted to strip her bare and conquer every inch of her. Sebastian wanted to see her entire body flush from his touch. *Had anyone else touched her like this? Had anyone else claimed her?* His possessiveness had him cursing the thought of any other man loving Penelope. But did he have a right to those thoughts?

Sebastian held Penelope's face as he gently brought his lips to hers once again. This time his kiss was sweet, tentative, reassuring. He needed to win her confidence and trust. He needed her to see what a fool he'd been, and know that he was willing to make up for his stupidity.

Would she give me that chance?

When he pulled back and Penelope opened her eyes, she looked dazed, questioning his actions. Before she had a chance to utter a sound, Sebastian spoke. "I won't say that was a mistake. Not this time." He watched Penelope's surprised expression. "Penelope, I was a fool. I'll never be able to say how sorry I was for causing you pain, but I'd like the chance to change that. I'll beg for your forgiveness if that's what it takes. I want another chance for your love."

"Bastian," Penelope whispered, closing her eyes.

He felt her body soften and relax against his. Sebastian's hands were still tangled in her hair. As her eyes opened again, he held her gaze. "Please, Penelope," he pleaded. "I won't hurt you again."

"I want to believe you, but how can I trust you?"

"You can," he rushed to say.

Penelope lifted her chin. "You hurt me, Sebastian. You broke my heart. With no explanation what so ever."

"I know, and I've regretted it all these years. So many times I wanted to come to you, call you, try again."

"What stopped you? Why did you turn me away?" A lone tear rolled down her face, nearly breaking Sebastian.

"We'll talk. Will you give me the chance to explain?" Sebastian continued to hold her head, his fingers gently massaging her scalp. He watched her eyes, watched the emotions; knew she was battling with herself as to what she should do. He couldn't let this chance slip away. "Penelope."

She opened her mouth to speak when a voice called out from behind Sebastian.

"Excuse me, Mr. Mauer?"

Penelope's eyes widened, and her cheeks reddened as Sebastian reluctantly pulled his hands away from her to face the person who had interrupted them. Sebastian was pretty sure that Penelope was embarrassed to be found in this situation with him, but he couldn't care less. His only thought was winning this woman over no matter the cost.

"Yes?" Sebastian addressed the woman standing before him, recognizing her as the administrator, Terri, who had informed the orchestra of LaPelle's illness.

Terri cleared her throat, her gaze darting quickly from Sebastian, to Penelope, and back to Sebastian again. "I've just spoken with Director LaPelle, and he has informed me that he'd like you to continue leading the rehearsals for the next few days while he tries to recover. He'll be calling you this evening after your scheduled interview with Ms. Beacham, if that's all right."

Sebastian raised his brow, wondering how word had already gotten back to LaPelle about today's rehearsal. His question was answered as Terri spoke again.

"He received several messages from Symphony members stating their excitement and encouragement for you when you led them today." She smiled. "He has the authority to voice his replacement, whether it's temporary or long-term."

"That's very gracious of him. And also of the members who supported me," Sebastian stated humbly. "I'll look forward to speaking with him tonight."

"Also, he'd like me to give you a copy of the key to his office, so that you may access his notes and music." She offered the key to Sebastian.

He reached out to take it then placed it in his pocket. "Thank you."

"You're welcome," she answered with a nod before leaving the couple.

Sebastian stood immobile, trying to process the turn of events this morning brought. He turned back to Penelope, hoping that where she was concerned, he'd also hear something positive.

She cleared her throat as the blush slowly receded from her cheeks. "You did very well, Sebastian. As if you'd been doing it forever."

"It nearly felt that way." He took a step closer to her.

"And that surprises you." She didn't question, she stated it, as if knowing his thoughts. Penelope stood straighter but didn't cower from his approach. He took that as a good sign.

Sebastian bent to retrieve Penelope's coat from the floor, offering it back to her. When she reached out to take it, his other hand came up to clasp hers and pull her into him. He was delighted with another startled gasp. "That's not all that surprises me," he whispered against her lips before brushing them with his. "You surprise me." He kissed. "You incite me." He nibbled. "And you'd humble me with another chance to prove my love for you." He swallowed her sigh as they melted into one another again, their kiss intensifying with each passing second.

Sebastian reluctantly broke their contact, wanting, needing to slow this down. Otherwise he'd already have her halfway to his room, anticipating so much more than just passionate kisses. But as much as he desired that, craved it, he knew he had to proceed with caution and care in order to win Penelope over. He couldn't afford to hurt her again and risk losing her for good. Hell, he wasn't even sure that he had her back yet, but he was damn sure going to give it his best shot.

"Penelope, what can I do to win your trust? To prove this is real?"

"I, I don't know, Sebastian," she hesitated. She tried to step back but Sebastian held tight. "You were so adamant about not having me, and now, now this onslaught of, of–"

"Physical demonstration of my desire?" he offered, his mouth quirking.

"You find this amusing? How can I take anything you do or say seriously?" She pushed at his chest, leaving him no choice but to release her, give her space; when in fact that was the last thing he truly wanted to do.

"I understand your hesitation, your indecision. I–"

"Do you?" her voice rose as scarlet bloomed again across her face. Only this time, Sebastian feared it was due to anger, not arousal. "You have no idea the emotional toil I've been through. The heartache, the second-guessing, the wondering what I could have possibly done wrong to make you turn away from me. I may have been young, naïve, and innocent, but I know what my heart felt. And I thought I knew what yours felt too."

"And now?" He hoped there was still some lingering emotion that he could ignite and use to take this relationship on the path he so wanted.

"And now I just don't know. You've already taken my heart on a roller coaster ride that I can't handle. I won't be hurt again." Her pleas tore at him.

"You won't, I promise that." Sebastian stepped toward her, only to have her side-step him and stay out of reach.

"Don't make promises," she said, taking another step away. "You can't guarantee anything, Sebastian." Her look of sadness was an arrow to his heart.

"I guarantee that I'll do my damnedest to make you believe in my love."

"Why now? Why after all this time?" she pleaded.

"Fate brought us back together for a reason. Don't we owe it to one another to find out why?"

"Fate," she scoffed. "And what if we hadn't encountered one another? What if I hadn't accepted this position? What if you hadn't been called to collaborate? Would you be seeking me out to prove your love for me?"

He knew the instant he'd made the mistake of hesitating that he was losing her. Would he have sought her out and tried again? Sebastian saw the hurt on her face once again and rushed to erase it. "I'd like to think so. I never stopped thinking about you. In fact, I-"

"Stop," she said quietly. "Just stop, Sebastian. You can't even be honest with yourself, because you just don't know. You claim to have loved me, yet you broke off our relationship and left me devastated. And here you are now, claiming to love me, to have made a mistake, and that you want to try again. Well I can't."

"Penelope." He stepped towards her but she recoiled.

"No." She shook her head. "Your words aren't enough. I don't know if they ever will be." She stepped around him and fled.

Sebastian watched her round the corner, not going after her this time.

If his words weren't enough, then his actions would have to be. He'd show her how much she meant to him and exactly what he'd do to win back her love. No matter the reason for them reuniting, he wasn't going to lose this second chance.

Chapter 11

Once again Penelope found herself running away from Sebastian, her heart hurting and her emotions a mess. She felt like a broken record and was damn tired of it!

"Time to take control of my life." She was talking to herself as she entered the Fairmont, not even noticing a few curious stares from passers-by. Walking directly to the spa, she decided to make appointments for herself and Lindsay to be pampered on Friday before the reception that evening.

As she strolled through the door, she was greeted by a lovely woman behind the counter. "Good afternoon, how may I help you?"

"Hello. I'd like to see if you have any appointments for Friday."

"What did you have in mind, Ms. Dixon?"

Penelope was surprised that the woman knew her name. As if on cue, the woman spoke again while giving her a pleasant smile.

"Yes, I know who you are, Ms. Dixon. You're the pianist with the Seattle Symphony and an esteemed guest here at the Fairmont. I'm Sophia, and I'd be happy to assist you."

"Oh, well, thank you. And please, call me Penelope. I'd like to schedule something for myself and my friend who's also a member of the symphony."

"Certainly." She pulled a brochure from beneath the counter and handed it to Penelope. "We have a variety of services, from facials and massages, to wraps, as well as hair and make-up."

Penelope took a moment to look over the information and settled on the *Indulge* spa package, which included a sauna treatment, massage and facial. The perfect combination she thought to unwind and feel truly spoiled. After booking the appointments for her and Lindsay, she thanked Sophia and headed up to her room. She considered another swim but thought better of it, not wanting to chance running into Sebastian should he have the same idea of finding her there again.

She knew she couldn't avoid him; they had a dinner and interview together this evening. Which reminded her, he had asked to speak with her about tonight. She wondered what had been on his mind. Obviously, he got distracted. Her hand went to her mouth as she remembered his desperate kiss that had startled yet excited her. Groaning at her weakness, she put aside those thoughts and decided to call her father. They'd spoken Sunday night when she arrived, although briefly, but she felt the need to talk with him. And, keeping in mind her conversation with LaPelle, she'd try to understand the reasoning for his actions in regards to her position with the Symphony.

Penelope knew her father loved her and she felt very fortunate for that love. She almost wanted to confess her feelings about Sebastian to him and finally have it out in the open, but knew it wasn't the right time.

Would it ever be?

After changing into more comfortable clothes, she settled into a lounge chair and dialed home. Two rings barely sounded when a familiar voice answered. "Dixon residence."

Penelope instantly smiled, imagining Gertie's face. A lovely woman in her late fifties, Gertie had managed the Dixon household for the past twenty years. She did everything from assisting Bernard and Penelope with their schedule and traveling, to hiring, firing, and commanding the other staffers. She was as close to a mother figure as Penelope had ever had.

"Gertie, it's so good to hear your voice."

"Penelope, it's wonderful to hear yours as well. How are you settling in, dear?"

"Fine. I've already made quite an impression with the Symphony and the director, and I've found a friend in one of the other younger members; a flautist named Lindsay."

"And how are you handling working with Sebastian Mauer?"

Penelope hadn't expected that question and floundered for something to say. Before she could compose an answer, Gertie spoke again.

"Don't think for a moment that just because you're out of this house, that you're out of my range of caring. I've made a point of reading all about the Seattle Symphony and their postings about you and Sebastian." Penelope couldn't get a word in edgewise as Gertie continued on. "And don't think for a moment that I wasn't aware of your relationship with that Sebastian Mauer. Now, Penelope Anne, tell me how you are doing? Has the man come to his senses, or do I need to arrange for his sudden disappearance?" She ended with a chuckle.

Penelope didn't know whether to laugh or cry. She did a bit of both as she poured out her soul to Gertie, telling her all that had transpired in only two days' time.

"Well, he may think he's come to his senses, but he has a lot to learn about wooing back the so-called love of his life," she huffed, clearly not impressed with Sebastian's actions either. "I so wish I was there to comfort you, dear," her tone softened, so full of love.

"Oh, Gertie, how I miss you. And Father, too." The thought of him suddenly had her wondering if he also knew of her feelings for Sebastian so long ago. "Gertie, I never confided in anyone years ago about what happened between me and Sebastian. Did Father know as well?"

"If he did, he never let on. He never once spoke to me about it, nor I to him. I suppose I foolishly thought that whatever took place had been dealt with, and you were fine. I see now how wrong that was." The sad tone to her voice was evident.

"It's not your fault. I was too embarrassed to talk about it. I suppose I just thought the hurt would pass as time went on. But time doesn't heal all pain." Penelope groaned. "What was I thinking coming to Seattle?"

"You were thinking that it was time to seek life on your own, and it was. It *is*. Penelope, life is full of many things, from challenges to wonderful experiences that only enhance our lives. You've done more at your young age than many do in an entire lifetime. But there's much more waiting for you, and unfortunately the road won't always be smooth."

"I've only begun to realize that. But I won't let Sebastian dictate what I do and how I feel. He may have broken my heart once, but I'll be damned if I'll let him do it again."

"Often times, the heart and the mind don't initially see eye-to-eye. But given time, you'll know what's best for you."

"Thank you, Gertie. I always knew you were intuitive, but you continue to surprise me."

"That's my job." She chuckled.

"How is father? Is he able to talk?"

"He's doing well, but he's not home at the moment. He should return in a few hours. Would you like me to ask him to call you when he does?"

"Actually, no, thank you. I'll be attending a dinner and interview this evening. It's for an article that will help promote the Symphony's upcoming performances."

"Well, I hope you have a pleasant evening and I'll look forward to reading the article. As will your father, I'm sure."

"Please give him my love. I'll try to call in a day or two."

"I'll do that, dear. You take care of yourself."

"You as well. I love you, Gertie."

There was a moment of pause before she answered. "I love you too, Penelope." Her voice was thick with emotion.

They didn't say good-byes, only disconnected their call. Penelope closed her eyes and let their conversation sink into her brain. *Smooth roads. Ha!* The last few days had been anything but, and Penelope knew it was her own choosing. Not that she'd chosen to be reunited with Sebastian in this fashion and have her emotions waver from one extreme to the other. However, she did choose this change in her life, and she was determined to make sure the path led to where *she* wanted to go.

Now, if she could just decide on the destination.

She laughed at herself and her thoughts as she jumped out of the chair. Time to stop wallowing. A yoga session seemed like the perfect distraction. Hopefully it would provide calm and help her refocus as she prepared for the evening ahead.

—

Sebastian closed down his laptop after exchanging emails with LaPelle, as well as sending one out to all the symphony members. The director had unfortunately lost his voice, and Sebastian was officially taking over the rehearsals until he was better. And, if it came to it, LaPelle had already asked him to consider being Interim Conductor for the performances.

He couldn't have been more thrilled. Sebastian never thought he'd actually look forward to being in the limelight again.

He had thoroughly enjoyed performing in the past for the pure joy of playing, never for the attention and accolades that some others sought. When the press began to run stories on him as his career grew, it seemed overwhelming and caused distractions from his music. He had been a man in his late twenties who was still discovering himself, refining his craft, and coming to terms with his talent and fame. Admittedly, Sebastian had been very mature in some aspects, but very immature in others. He had no patience for what he viewed at the time as senseless interviews about his family, what he did in his spare time, and gee, what would his ideal woman be like?

Sebastian had always been a private person. He had been raised by his mother and had known nothing of his father while growing up, yet he never felt as if anything was missing from his life. His mother, Daphine Mauer, gave him everything he could have ever needed; most importantly, love, compassion, and constant encouragement for his music. And although Sebastian gained fortune, it hadn't changed the two of them or their relationship with one another.

It did, however, cause his father to suddenly come out of the so-called woodwork, seeking a part of that fortune. Daphine had confessed that although he knew of the pregnancy, he had wanted no part of it all those years ago; and that she and Sebastian were better off for it.

Imagine the gall of that man, extorting money from him? Sebastian had and would only refer to him as a donor. Petty, he knew, but he had no emotions for him whatsoever.

Sebastian had dealt with that at the same time that he and Penelope had met all those years ago. And, although they did their best to keep their budding relationship a secret, he knew it'd only be a matter of time before not only the press got wind of it, but his donor as well. As he and his mother initially struggled to deal with it, he thought it best to break things off with Penelope until he could control the situation and ultimately eliminate the problem. The last thing he wanted for Penelope and her father was to get pulled into the fiasco that had suddenly become his life.

Hence the halting of his performances, with no ties whatsoever to the media, no public outings, and no explanation to Penelope. And yes, their age difference had been a concern as well. He had foolishly thought that Penelope had needed more time to mature and experience life, and he had every intention of explaining things to Penelope when the time was right.

Unfortunately, it had been Sebastian himself who had needed maturing, and as the months and years passed, the time had never felt right. It had taken longer than anticipated, and certainly longer than Sebastian would have liked to deal with his donor, once the law and proper legal channels were used. During that time, he had watched Penelope bloom and her career with her father soar. He no longer felt worthy. Never once did he consider the pain he had caused; not realizing at the time the depth of her feelings for him. Nor his for her.

Instead, he had carried on, thinking that she'd moved on with her life as well.

Until their lives had intersected again, and it was perfectly clear that those feelings had only been dampened, just waiting to be sparked anew. Sebastian had to find a way to explain everything to Penelope and pray to God that she'd give him another chance.

Putting aside those thoughts for now, he took the time to call his mother, wanting to check in on her and see how Samson and Delilah were doing.

"Sebastian!" she greeted. "How are you?"

"Hi, Mom. I'm fine, and you? How are you holding up with the twins?"

"Oh, you know I love Samson and Delilah, and look forward to keeping them whenever you decide to travel." Shuffling and barking sounded in the background, followed by a slamming door. "Yes, yes, all right you two. I'm talking to your daddy. Here you go." After a pause, she continued. "I just gave them treats and was about to join them for a romp around the yard. They're playing in the mud and loving it!"

"Don't tell me you're going to stomp in the mud puddles too?" he asked with a chuckle. He knew his mother wasn't afraid of getting dirty. She gardened and did pottery, and lately had started to experiment with wood working.

"I just might!" She joked. "Now, tell your mother how you're really doing. As much as I love talking to you, you've only been gone a few days, so it's a little early for your check-in," she teased. "Is it Penelope?"

His mother always knew how to get to the heart of the matter. There'd been no hiding his feelings for Penelope from her. She had even encouraged him to be honest with Penelope from the start and keep their relationship going, but his stubbornness got in the way.

"Yes," he answered.

"And?" she prodded. "What happened?"

"*She* happened. She only had to walk into the room," he said with a wistful tone to his voice. "Penelope is lovelier than ever. Her playing is extraordinary. She is truly a beautiful person—"

"Whom you now must convince to love you again," she finished for him.

"How do you do that?"

"Do what?" she asked innocently.

"Know exactly the situation without even being present."

"My dear, Sebastian, I'm your mother. I know you. I also know the love you had for her, and I'm assuming still do; but you broke her heart and now you must mend it."

"I didn't realize all those years ago what I had done. To both of us. Such a fool," he mumbled. "But seeing her again, knowing that there are still feelings–"

"Feelings you must be careful with. She may still feel for you, but she has to trust you first."

He sighed. "Yes, that's exactly what she said."

"Oh, so you two have had a chance to talk?"

Sebastian half-heartedly chuckled even though nothing about his encounters with Penelope was even remotely funny. "No, I wouldn't exactly call what we've done, talking."

"Sebastian, explain," she demanded.

He took a deep breath and launched into it, telling his mother of first seeing Penelope during the rehearsal, their awkward "hellos" and meeting with LaPelle. Then of course, the unfortunate episodes at the pool and in her room that had him questioning his own sanity as well as cursing himself again for the pain he'd caused.

"Sebastian Xavier Mauer! How could you? It's no wonder that poor girl is completely confused and suspicious. You've really got your work cut out for you if you hope to win her love again."

"I know. And I do. Hope to win her back, that is. I can't believe what an idiot I was."

Daphine quickly interjected. "Well, I can. As much as I love you, you were and still are a stubborn, prideful man. Sebastian, you had no clue all those years ago. Your infatuation was strong, but distance has truly made your heart grow fonder. With time came maturity, even if there was heartbreak. Hopefully it's not too late to repair that for you two. You need to find that balance between conveying your love and giving Penelope the needed space to figure this out for herself as well.

"Now, as a mother who would love to fix everything for her son, that's all the advice I'll give you. The twins are getting restless so I'm going to go and make sure they get their walk."

Just as she finished, Sebastian heard whimpers and barking, indicating that Samson and Delilah were indeed antsy and ready for action.

"All right, Mother, thank you. I'll talk to you in a few days."

"I love you, Sebastian."

"I love you too."

They disconnected, leaving Sebastian with much to contemplate. Balance, patience, restraint; even humility – qualities he knew he had to have if he was going to be successful in pursuing Penelope and making her a part of his life again.

"It all begins tonight," he said as he began to change for the dinner and interview. He and Penelope were due to meet the reporter, Kimberly Beacham in The Georgian Restaurant in less than an hour, which didn't give him much time for a little surprise he wanted to arrange first.

After dressing quickly he made his way downstairs to begin his campaign.

Chapter 12

Penelope approached the restaurant ready to give her name to the hostess when she was greeted first instead.

"Good evening, Ms. Dixon. If you'll please follow me, I'll take you to your party."

Penelope nodded before following the woman, still not sure what to make of being so easily recognized lately. With only five minutes to spare, Sebastian and Ms. Beacham must surely be there by now. As she was led through the open, elegant dining room, she scanned the area looking for them. She grew concerned when she didn't spot them and continued to be led away from the main dining area.

The hostess stopped at a closed door, the plaque on the wall indicating the name of the room was *The Petite*. Unable to hide her surprise, she asked why a private room.

"Mr. Mauer arranged for the room. He's inside waiting. I'll escort Ms. Beacham in when she arrives."

"Oh, she's not here yet?"

"No, ma'am. She phoned to say that she was unavoidably delayed, but shouldn't be much longer."

"Thank you." As the hostess nodded and turned to walk away, Penelope drew in a breath. She instantly became anxious, unsure if she could handle even a few moments alone with the man right now. Would he be reserved and aloof? Or would he continue his pursuit, insisting on a second chance? And how much longer could she keep her guard up?

Yes, she could admit that she still had feelings for Sebastian. Were those feelings of love? Infatuation? All these years apart had changed them both and she needed to figure out if giving them another chance was worth it. If it was what she really wanted.

Her earlier conversation with Gertie echoed in her mind. No more weakness; no more broken hearted. Time to dictate her future.

Penelope grasped the door handle and entered the room. What she saw took her breath away!

Daffodils and hyacinths filled the room in a variety of vases and containers that were placed along the center table, side tables, and floating shelves. In the middle of it all stood Sebastian, never looking better in black slacks and jacket with a crisp, white shirt beneath, holding a white tulip in his hand.

Perched on the threshold, all Penelope could do was stare in astonishment. As she drank in the site of the beautiful flowers, along with the confident look on Sebastian's face, she finally registered his movement toward her.

"Please, come in, Penelope." He extended his hand that held the tulip, and as she released the door to accept it, he took that opportunity to lead her further into the room and close the door behind her. "Hello," he whispered as he leaned in to place a soft kiss on her temple. "You look beautiful."

When he stepped back, she took a moment to study his face, his eyes, and knew she could easily lose herself in them. "Thank you," she said, looking away. She had dressed in cream slacks and a cranberry cashmere sweater, adding pearl studs to her ears that were a gift from Gertie.

Looking around the room, she commented, "These flowers are amazing. What is all this for?"

"For you." When she swung her gaze to him, he continued. "My way off asking your forgiveness. These flowers are not only beautiful, but they represent a way to say I'm sorry and ask that you forgive me."

"You did all this for me?"

"You're worth it and more, Penelope." He leaned closer, almost nuzzling her neck as he whispered, "So much more."

It took all the strength she had not to turn in his arms and let him sweep her away. When she stepped away, she started to speak. "Sebastian-"

Keyed Up

"Don't say anything. Not yet. Let's enjoy this evening." He stepped to the table and pulled out a chair for her. "Please, sit. I'll pour us some wine while we wait for Ms. Beacham."

Only then did she notice two wine bottles on the table, along with a pitcher of water and an assortment of what looked like appetizers.

"You arranged for all of this as well?" she asked as she sat in the chair he offered, still holding the tulip in her hand.

"I did. I took the liberty of ordering the food and wine. Would you care for white or red?"

"White, please." She noticed it was a Riesling, one of her favorites. "Were you aware that Ms. Beacham was going to be late?"

He nodded. "I was informed. But knowing your punctuality, I knew I didn't have time to waste. The staff here and at the floral shop were most accommodating. Their efforts were excellent." He grinned as he placed the wine glass in front of her.

"Yes, and I'm sure you being Sebastian Mauer had nothing what so ever to do with their expediency," she grinned in return as she lifted the glass. Sebastian kept his eyes on her as she savored the sweetness of the wine. She delighted in seeing his eyes narrow slightly as she licked her lips before returning the glass to the table.

He straightened and cleared his throat. "And I'm sure I have no idea what you mean by that." His smile was breathtaking.

She watched him pour another glass of the Riesling, along with water in three glasses as he remained standing on her side of the table. His movements were efficient and shouldn't have been so sexy. Still, Penelope couldn't help the flush she felt creeping into her cheeks. She lifted the glass for another sip, hoping to disguise her nervousness. Ensuring that her voice would be steady, she questioned Sebastian about this evening.

"You had mentioned that you wanted to talk about this interview."

"Yes, before I got distracted." Instead of sitting, he leaned back against the table, studying her. His heated gaze caused her entire body to warm, wishing she'd chosen a blouse to wear instead of the sweater. "I wondered what you may want to reveal about our past when those questions arise, because I can assure you, they will. I've done my research on Kimberly Beacham, and while she does have an excellent reputation and her articles are concise, she does her research as well. I'm positive she'll bring up our connection, considering my collaborations with your father."

Penelope too, had wondered about this topic, but admittedly pushed it aside. Now, it was time to face the dilemma. She wasn't ashamed of her past relationship with him, but was *he*? She certainly didn't want her father to learn of their relationship via an article instead of from his own daughter. And really, what did their past have to do with the present? They weren't a couple – although if Sebastian's expressed desires had any bearing in the matter, they certainly would be back together soon.

"Nothing about our relationship was public as we managed to keep it private; even from my father. I don't see that there's anything to mention, except that I came to know you by way of you working with Father."

"I see," he said, his voice laced with disappointment.

Well what did he expect? A sudden change of heart? He's done nothing to really prove a change in himself. Although his words –

Her thoughts were interrupted by the door opening and a lovely young woman entering. Penelope assumed it was Kimberly, who clearly looked surprised as she took in the scene.

"Oh, hello. I didn't realize the interview would be so intimate." Her rounded eyes were warm and brown, and honey blond hair cascaded over her shoulders. She wore caramel slacks and a jacket with a cream blouse underneath.

Sebastian pushed away from the table and turned to welcome her. "I thought it'd be more enjoyable and productive to have some privacy. Crowds are distracting. Please, have a seat," he offered as he held out a chair at the head of the table. A table capable of seating a dozen people. Once she was seated he offered to pour her some wine.

"Red, please."

After he placed the wine glass in front of her, he walked to the opposite side of the table, placing himself across from Penelope.

"Thank you," Kimberly said, settling her belongings on the table. "And please excuse my late arrival." She turned to Penelope. "Even though we know of each other, introductions are both professional and courteous." She extended her hand to Penelope. "Kimberly

Beacham, but please, call me Kim."

"Penelope Dixon. Penelope," she said as she placed the tulip she'd been holding the entire time on the table. She smiled and returned Kim's handshake.

When the reporter turned to Sebastian, he stood, offering his hand and greeting. "Sebastian. A pleasure to meet you."

Penelope noticed Kim's easy smile. "Believe me, the pleasure is mine. Meeting you both and having you agree to an interview is wonderful, so thank you."

"We're happy to promote the Symphony's work," Penelope added.

"And your debut here," Kim said. "You must be thrilled. Any nervousness?"

Penelope chuckled. "Not any longer. I love to play, and in the few days I've been here, I've made a great connection with the orchestra."

"Do you mind if I run my audio recorder? I don't want to make the mistake of not remembering anything from this evening."

"I have no objections," Penelope stated. "Sebastian?"

"None. And please, help yourself to the food. Let's make this as pleasurable as possible. Would either of you care to order anything other than the appetizers?"

"No, no, thank you. This is very gracious of you," Kim replied.

"And there's plenty," Penelope added. "I'm fine with what's here."

Sebastian nodded and lifted his wine for a drink.

"All right then, may I launch into some questions?" Kim asked.

"Certainly," Sebastian replied as Penelope said yes.

"What's the occasion for all the flowers?" she asked as she looked around the room. She set her recorder on the table after turning it on. "Or is this room always decorated this way? They're beautiful."

Penelope looked at Sebastian, hesitating to answer.

"An early birthday surprise for Penelope, as well as a welcoming to the Symphony," Sebastian offered. "I have it on good authority that she loves flowers."

"And what woman wouldn't." Kim laughed. "Well, happy early birthday, Penelope. April seventh, correct?"

"Why, yes," she answered, a little surprised. Although Sebastian had said that Kim does her research.

"And not long after your opening night. How exciting." She took a sip of her water before placing a few appetizers on a plate. "Hope either of you don't mind if I help myself? It's been a while since lunch."

"Not at all. I'm ready for something as well." Sebastian made his selection, asking Penelope if she was going to eat.

"Yes, thank you." Penelope placed her choices on a plate, watching the dynamics unfold.

"So, Penelope," Kim began between dainty bites of her prawns. "How do you feel about your first debut without your father?"

"Well, as I said, I've made a great connection with the orchestra and am delighted to work with them. I admit I was nervous at first, wondering if I would be accepted, but-"

"Why would you think you wouldn't be accepted?" Kim interrupted.

"I suppose acceptance isn't the correct word, given that every one of the members are professionals and would perform to the best of their abilities no matter what. Rapport would be a better descriptor. With joining the symphony at this late date, I've not had the chance to build a rapport with the orchestra. These members have worked together for months, many, for years; so as a newcomer it can be a bit challenging. Especially with our performance only weeks away."

"Do you think the fact that you're Bernard Dixon's daughter played to your advantage, or did that add more trepidation?"

"I've never used my father as a bargaining chip," she said with a bit more edge to her voice than she intended. "I guess I felt the need to prove myself; to prove that I am more than Bernard Dixon's daughter. I was pleased when informed that my position here was due strictly to my own talents. As for not being alongside my father, while we had a wonderful touring career, I was ready for another phase. And father was ready to slow down."

"Is he retiring altogether?"

"Not yet. He's limited his engagements and reduced his overseas travel dramatically."

"And do you hope to continue to travel and make appearances elsewhere?"

"I wouldn't say no to travel, but I'd love to enjoy more personal time when I do. For now I'm committed to the Seattle Symphony through this season, which ends in July. Then it'll be decided if they'd like me to continue."

"And would *you* like to continue?"

"At this point, I'd say yes, as I haven't made any other plans or had any other offers."

Kim turned to Sebastian. "And you, Sebastian, coming out of hiding, so-to-speak, to debut your latest work. Why after all these years? You've worked closely with Penelope's father, Bernard, but remained out of the public eye. Did knowing that Penelope would be with the symphony influence your decision?"

"In part, yes."

His answer shouldn't have shocked her, given his recent adamant plea for their reunion. Never the less, her insides still fluttered at his admission.

"Working with Bernard over the years was an experience that I'm forever grateful for. I had my reasons for staying away from performing, for staying away from the media. I dealt with a very personal, troublesome situation, and felt my decisions at the time were for the best. And as hindsight would have it, it turns out that I was wrong."

Sebastian's gaze bore into Penelope, as if his confession were for her alone. Her eyes stayed locked with his, riveted by the emotions they displayed; intrigued by the expressions on his face.

"Would you care to elaborate on that subject?" Kim asked quietly. She glanced back and forth between Penelope and Sebastian.

"I would." He kept his gaze on Penelope. "As fate would have it, Bernard called me, enticing me with this collaboration. I had an unspoken debt to repay him." When her eyes widened in question, he continued. "Only a day later, LaPelle called, inviting me to work with the Symphony. Of course I could have turned them down, but knew it was time."

"Time to make a public appearance again?"

"Among other things."

What "other" things? Did he really want to see me again? If so, why –

Kim spoke again. "Can you tell me about your composition? It's been nearly two years since your last, according to my sources. What inspired this piece for you?"

He turned to Kim and answered. "I began this piece years ago, inspired by love, its loss, and the regret that followed." He turned back to Penelope. "Only recently have I come to realize the result of knowing true love, having lost it, and wishing by any means to obtain it again."

Penelope was breathless. Her hand stilled as it reached for her wine glass. The conviction in his voice arrowed through her; pierced her heart. If she had doubts about Sebastian's true feeling before, they were beginning to fade.

"Bastian." When she saw his eyes soften and a smile take shape on his lips, Penelope realized she'd spoken his name. Out of her periphery, she saw Kim's head swing her way. There was no way the reporter wouldn't have picked up on the connection between her and Sebastian. The question now was how much more was she ready to have revealed?

Sebastian answered. "Kim, you may have surmised that my composition was inspired by Penelope. A fact she wasn't aware of until now. And while she may not be ready for this confession to be made public, I want there to be no question about my feelings for her.

"I love her."

Chapter 13

The silence that followed was like a vacuum, sucking all of the air from the room. Sebastian was all in now. He would divulge every truth and show Penelope his intentions were honest in gaining her faith in him again.

"How long have you loved her?" Kim asked.

"Since the first moment I saw her, ten years ago, New Year's Eve in Vienna. She took my breath away. But being twenty-eight and she barely eighteen, it seemed inappropriate."

"Love knows no bounds," Penelope whispered, her memories taking her back to that blissful night.

"That may be, but I felt I was looking out for your reputation. And," he hesitated, looking down at the wine glass he twirled with his fingers. "There was another matter that I didn't want you and Bernard to be a part of."

"What, Sebastian? What was it that you couldn't share?" Penelope pleaded, unconcerned now about Kimberly's presence.

"My father," he stated without looking up.

"What about your father?" she questioned. "I don't understand. You told me you were raised by your mother, never knowing anything about your father."

"There's nothing in my research about your father," Kim spoke up.

Sebastian looked at Kim. "That's because I went to great lengths to ensure that." He then turned to Penelope. "It's true my mother raised me, and she gave me everything I ever needed; ever wanted. She told me that we were better off not having my father in our lives. When I began to gain my so-called fame and fortune, he thought otherwise." Sebastian paused and took a breath before continuing.

"My father knew of my mother's pregnancy, but wanted nothing to do with raising a child. They were twenty-three year old hippies – my mother's words – and he had plenty of living to do that didn't include taking care of a baby. So he went on his merry way while she raised me. Then, after all those years, it seemed he felt the need to worm his way back into my life and demand money from me."

"What on earth gave him the right to think that you owed him anything when he was the one who abandoned you and your mother? He failed as a father; as a decent human being. Why not just ignore him? What could he have possibly done to either of you?" Penelope's defense of Sebastian warmed him and gave him hope.

"He harassed us, caused inconveniences in our lives. He thought he could threaten me by going to the press with false stories about us. And although he had nothing damning, it was affecting my work, and the last thing I wanted was for the press to gain any information to run with. False or not. For a man who didn't make much of his life, he sure went to great lengths to extort me and make my life, as well as my mother's, miserable.

"But most importantly, Mother's safety came into question. His threats began to take a bad turn, and the authorities were finally called in. By the time it was dealt with and he was arrested, it'd been nearly two years."

"Oh, Sebastian."

Penelope radiated sympathy, but he didn't want sympathy; he wanted her understanding and her forgiveness.

He shook his head. "I couldn't let you get dragged into that, Penelope. Your career would have suffered, maybe even Bernard's. I wasn't about to let that happen. Hell, if given the choice, I'm sure you would have kept your distance from me anyway."

"But you didn't give me that choice, did you? You just assumed I was a young, naïve girl who would've walked away."

Sebastian and Penelope volleyed back and forth while Kim sat back and watched.

"I had every intention of contacting you again once the situation was dealt with, but you seemed to have moved on with your life."

"Again, because you gave me no choice," she enunciated each word. "What was I supposed to do, pine for you until you thought it the right time? Until *you* thought it convenient? Or until enough time had passed that you thought I may have matured enough?"

Sebastian pushed away his wine and clasped his hands together on top of the table. "I had no idea it would take the time that it did. I was trying to spare you and your father any ugliness in your life."

Penelope lurched to her feet, startling Kim. "Oh stop, Sebastian. If you had truly cared for me, felt the love that I thought you did – because believe me, I *thought* I loved *you* – you would have trusted me. At the very least, you should have trusted Father. He was deeply saddened by your withdrawal."

Sebastian was surprised by her statement. "He never mentioned anything about–"

"Of course he didn't," she interrupted. "He thought you would confide in him, given the level of friendship the two of you had built. Father wasn't about to pry; in his eyes that wasn't proper. But in hind sight, he'd wished he had. I wasn't the only one who missed you. Even with your long distance relationship, it wasn't the same. Father was never the same." Penelope gave him an assessing look as she cocked her head. "Didn't you realize that with all of Father's constant requests for you to visit, to collaborate – and not via long-distance – that he was reaching out to you?"

At Sebastian's stunned silence, Penelope crossed her arms and jumped in again. "No, you didn't. And I never confided to him the love that I felt for you because it seemed it would only add to his sadness. Believe me, I'm no martyr, but I carried my burden and my hurt alone. Partly because I was stunned and ashamed at your dismissal, and partly because I wanted to spare Father the burden of more hurt as well. Maybe I should have though. Maybe he would have gotten brave enough for the both of us to confront you. Or mad enough.

"Either way, we didn't turn to one another as we should have. And do I blame you? At times I did, but I also realized it was my responsibility to own up to my feelings. I learned a difficult lesson and I told myself that I wouldn't be put in that position again. So thank you, Sebastian, for teaching me a lesson; for playing a part in my maturity." Her sarcasm was like a slap across his face.

Sebastian had meant for this to be his opportunity to admit to his mistakes of the past and to begin with a clean slate with Penelope. He quickly saw that opportunity slipping away. Not only had he hurt her, but Bernard as well. He never realized the depth of their friendship, and he had taken it for granted.

Before he could speak, Penelope lowered her arms and turned to Kim.

"Kim, I realize I have no control over what you put in your article, but I would request that none of our personal issues be brought up, as they have no relevance with promoting the Symphony and the upcoming performances. My past relationship with Sebastian is just that – in the past. We are collaborating in a professional capacity. If you feel the need to mention the inspiration for his composition, I would request that you not mention me being that inspiration. Because at this point, I'm having a hard time truly believing that."

"Penelope." He tried to interject, but she held up her hand for him to stop.

"I would request that you state I am honored to have been selected for the Symphony and am very much looking forward to finishing out a successful season. The lineup that we have planned can and should be enjoyed by all. I'll leave you my email should you have any further questions." At that point, Penelope gave her email address, knowing that Kim could refer back to her recording. "It was a pleasure meeting you. I'm sure you weren't prepared to be witness to all that transpired here. I can certainly say I was surprised; although it did answer questions that have lingered for many years. At that, I'm going to say good night. Enjoy the rest of your evening."

Penelope turned to Sebastian, giving him a cool stare. "I will see you in the morning for rehearsal." She quickly made her way to the door and out of the room.

Sebastian didn't have a chance to say another word to discourage her exit. He sat speechless, still trying to process how his plan had gone nothing like he had envisioned.

Kim leaned forward to pick up her recorder and turn it off. "One thing's for sure," she started, "she knows how to maintain her politeness."

Sebastian stared at the reporter, watching as the corner of her mouth quirked. He couldn't hold back the laugh that erupted, which was quickly followed by Kim's.

"Heaven forbid Penelope Dixon should be anything less than polite."

"She did show some teeth though, you have to admit," Kim added.

"That she did." Sebastian picked up his wine glass and emptied the contents in one swallow. He should not have been surprised at her conviction and backbone; those qualities were certainly admired.

"She seems to have given you quite a bit to chew on."

"You sure have a way with words," Sebastian quipped.

She shrugged a shoulder. "It's what I do." She grinned then took a healthy sip of her red wine, the food all but forgotten. "So, what's next?" When Sebastian gave her a quizzical look, she continued. "I'd say you have to change your strategy. Your pursuit of Penelope Dixon just got a bit more complicated."

"That's an understatement if I ever heard one." He sighed and ran his hand over his head, ruffling his hair. "At this point, I honestly have no idea."

"Well you can't give up. If you love her as much as you claim you do, then you keep trying."

"And when does my trying push the limits into harassment? I think she made it perfectly clear what she thought of me and my pursuit."

"I don't think she did anything of the sort. She was understandably angry, and probably a little disappointed in you. I think she just issued you a much more complicated challenge. Not only do you need to make amends with her, but with Bernard as well."

"Something I'm ashamed I never took into consideration. Mother was correct; I am a stubborn, prideful, idiotic man."

"Wow, and she claims to love you?" Kim chuckled.

"That she does. Lucky me." Sebastian smiled, but it faded quickly. "Kim, I apologize. As Penelope said, I'm sure this was not how you imagined the evening would go. I selfishly thought I could use this opportunity, this platform to declare my love, state my sins, and be forgiven."

"Nothing is that easy with us women."

"Clearly, I'm finding that out the hard way." He reached for the bottle of wine and poured another glass. Normally, Sebastian didn't drink often, but tonight he felt the need to stray from that norm. "Would you care for any more wine?"

"No, I haven't even finished my first glass. I'm not much of a drinker."

"Well neither am I, in case you couldn't tell." He raised the glass for a healthy drink.

"I must say, you're actually pretty calm about the whole thing. I'm surprised you aren't chasing her down, beating at her door to explain more."

"I'm afraid it would do no good. I think I need to give her time and space until I can reformulate my game plan."

"Good thinking. Some advice? Have all these flowers sent up to her room. Stay patient, but vigilant. Show her you aren't giving up while also giving her, her space."

"Balance."

"Exactly." Kim reached for her recorder and turned it on again. "Would you mind if I have your email? I'll draft my article and send it to you and Penelope for your perusal."

"Really? You'd actually let us dictate what you put in your article?"

"To a certain extent. I want to continue to build my reputation and my career. You may not have had much love for the media in the past, but I hope to change your perspective. The last thing I want is to make enemies out of public figures such as yourself and Penelope. You've done nothing to earn any ill press. My job is to promote the Symphony and the presence of you both; not to stir up gossip and conjecture."

Sebastian was taken aback by her admission. He expressed his respect and gratitude. "Thank you for that, Kim. I can't tell you how much I appreciate your honesty and your integrity."

"You're welcome. So, your email?" She held the recorder out closer to him, to which he spoke into. She then turned it off and placed it in her bag. "I thank you for the wine and food. I'm sorry much of it went untouched."

Sebastian waved away her concerns. "C'est la vie." He stood as Kim made a move to do the same. "I'll look forward to reading the article. Again, thank you. I do hope you enjoy the rest of the evening."

"I will. I'm actually just heading home to put the finishing touches on another article and then I'll get started on this one for the Symphony."

They both exited the room with Sebastian escorting Kim through the restaurant and to the front entrance.

"Good luck, Sebastian."

"I'll need that and more. Good night, Kim."

She nodded and walked away, leaving Sebastian to consider his next step. He walked to the front desk and made arrangements for the flowers from the meeting room to be sent up to Penelope. Once that was taken care of, his next thought was to call Bernard for a long-awaited heart-to-heart conversation.

Before going up to his room, he went back to the room to get one vase that held both daffodils and hyacinths and placed the white tulip inside. This one he'd take to the recital hall to place on the piano for Penelope.

He intended to make even small gestures count.

Chapter 14

Penelope was angry and confused. If she *were* more of a demonstrative person she may have been likely to punch holes in the wall. Once in her room, she took a few moments to calm herself before she did anything irrational. She sent a quick text to Lindsay telling her that the interview was enlightening and that she'd fill her in in the morning. Lindsay then suggested they meet before practice at the Starbucks around 8 AM, giving them plenty of time to talk. Penelope agreed and then apologized for not wanting to discuss any more this evening; instead, wanting to call and talk to her father.

Lindsay: Alright; C U in the AM. Have a good night!

Penelope: Good night

Penelope then phoned her father. After several rings, he finally picked up.

"Penelope, I didn't expect to hear from you this evening. Gertie said you had an interview scheduled."

"Hello Father. I did, and it's over. Sebastian and I met with Ms. Kimberly Beacham from Seattle Magazine."

"And how did it go? Plenty of good press for you two and the Symphony?"

"That is the hope. Although the interview did not go at all as I had imagined." She sighed and plopped down in the lounge chair.

"Oh? How so?" He sounded wary.

"Father, I have a confession." Might as well get right to it, she thought. "I hadn't planned to inform you in this manner, over the phone, and would rather have preferred to be face-to-face, but since that isn't possible at this time, and I don't wish to wait any longer, I'm just going to say it." She had a tendency to ramble when nervous, and her speech always became much more proper when speaking with her father.

"Penelope, what is it? You've got your dear old dad worried." Penelope thought he tried to sound light-hearted, but that really wasn't in Bernard's nature. He had always been a very matter-of-fact person.

"I don't know if you were ever aware of this, and if you were, you never let on that you were, so… I was in love with Sebastian, and fear that I still am. Although with his actions, not only in the past, but tonight especially, I question my sanity in that matter, and–"

"Penelope," Bernard interrupted her rambling. "I was aware," he said softly.

It took Penelope a moment for that to sink in before she uttered, "You were? And you never spoke to me about it?"

"At the time, I thought you were mature enough to know what you were doing, what you felt."

"Obviously you were the only one," she muttered.

"It took me a while to figure it out and I didn't want to get overly excited. I couldn't have been happier that the two of you were developing a…connection. When Sebastian called off his visits, citing personal issues and you went away to New England, I suspected something had happened. And then with your return, you were different, yet you carried on. I'm afraid I assumed that the relationship just didn't work out between you two and you were moving on with your life."

"And yet you were still willing to work professionally with him."

"Well, yes," he answered, surprise lacing his words. "Just because one relationship doesn't work out, doesn't mean one in a different capacity cannot. I mean, he began to excel at composing, and a performer is always looking for new material. A professional relationship such as that shouldn't be cast aside. I felt fortunate to still have that connection to him. It didn't mean I loved you any less."

"Oh no, Father. It wasn't my intention to question your loyalty to me just because you wanted to continue your professional connection to him. I am just amazed at how gracious a person you are. And I wished Sebastian had realized that those years ago."

"I am forever sorry that I was not more open with you. Perhaps I took for granted the maturity you gained at such a young age, never realizing that you truly didn't have a childhood. Nor the guidance of a mother." Now sorrow was evident in his voice.

"Father, you have nothing at all to be sorry for. I should apologize myself for not confiding in you in the first place. And then for not talking to you about how *you* felt when Sebastian stopped the visits, because I know it affected you as well. You two had grown very close. It seemed a part of you had withdrawn. And besides you, I had Gertie. Although she's not my mother, she filled that void wonderfully. I should have taken more advantage of that."

"All very true. I take it there were some confessions at this interview tonight?"

Penelope sighed. "Yes. Sebastian confessed his love for me and his desire to win me back. He explained what took place in his past to make him stop his visits and withdraw from the public. And at the time, he was still concerned about our age difference." Penelope went on to regale her father with Sebastian's story about his biological father and the reasoning for his decisions.

Bernard responded. "Seems all three of us have something to learn about opening up to those we love. After all, we're meant to support and nurture one another. Life was never meant to be accomplished alone." After hesitating for a moment, he continued. "So, what was your response to his confession? And to his desire to win back your love?"

"I was shocked, angry, let down. He didn't trust me with a decision that affected both of us. He jeopardized our relationship then severed it. And he hurt you as well in the process."

"Bah, we old men don't get our feelings hurt."

"Father, don't gloss over the discomfort you went through. I made Sebastian realize the extent of hurt and distrust he caused. I may still have feelings for him, but that doesn't mean I'm ready to reconcile. I need to process everything and decide where to go from here. I'm going to dictate what happens in my life. No one else."

"Penelope, I want you to know just how proud of you I am. You've always been mature beyond your years, but I'll apologize again for not being there as a father should have been when it came to you being in love."

"Father, don't berate yourself. You have given me a wonderful, fulfilling life. And because of that I am able to pursue my heart's desire. There's still much for me to learn and I will get there, but that's what life is about, right? The journey."

"Very true. So, where will your journey take you? Will you remain with the Symphony?"

"Oh, of course! In the few days' time, I've come to like it here and the connections I'm making. I will be ever the professional and suck it up, as they say, and work with Sebastian without question."

"That's my girl. No backing down." His chuckle carried across the distance to warm her heart.

"No." She chuckled along with him. "Father." Her tone became more serious. "I was told by LaPelle how you tried to use your influence to ensure my position here." When he tried to interrupt, she continued on. "No, let me just say that while at first I was hurt, thinking that I didn't get the position by my own merit, LaPelle assured me that I did. And, he made me see that what you did was out of love and concern. So with that said, did you possibly have any part in pulling Sebastian and me back together?" From Sebastian's earlier words, she had suspected, but wanted to hear from her father himself.

"I confess that I did. As I said, knowing of your love for him, and thinking – hoping – that he still loved you after all this time, I wanted there to be a chance for you both to come together again. With you moving into a new phase of your career, your life, I did not want you to be alone. You never took an interest in anyone else, and maybe I assumed that you could love no one other than Sebastian. I wanted a chance for you to be happy again. I see that that may not have been the wisest choice."

"I understand your concern, and what you did *was* out of love. I admit I do still have feelings for him, but am unsure where they'll go."

"They must start with forgiveness. Open your heart and mind to the truth."

"If only it were that easy."

"Penelope, I am sorry for *your* sorrow. I–"

"No father, it's not your fault. I'll get through this."

"I know you will."

"Should Sebastian call *you*, what would you say to him?"

"First, I would listen to what he had to say. Sebastian is not a malevolent person, and I truly believe, from what you've told me, he thought he was doing what was best. Now I'm not saying that causing you hurt in the process was something he chose to happen. It just did. And as unfortunate as it was, one must move on."

"And the hurt he caused you?"

"My dear Penelope, I am not a thin-skinned man who cried because my friend no longer wanted to play." He chuckled again.

Penelope laughed at her father's words, never before hearing such wit and comic relief come from him. "I rather like this side of you."

"Yes, well, life isn't meant to be taken too seriously."

"You certainly have a lot of life lessons today."

"And here's one more; with age comes reflection. Now, if Sebastian were to call, I suspect we would talk like gentlemen and remain the friends we have always been. Would I accept any apology that he had to offer? I'm sure I would. Would I look forward to possibly spending more time in his company? Absolutely."

"I'll say it again; you're a very gracious man, Father and I love you to no end."

"I love you, my dear Penelope. Gertie and I will look forward to seeing you in a few weeks' time for your debut."

"I will look forward to that as well."

"Good -, Ah, speak of the devil. I'm getting another call; from Sebastian."

"Oh, well, that was fast. Good luck, Father. I'll let you go so that you can speak with him. Good night."

"Good night, Penelope."

With that, they disconnected, leaving Penelope to contemplate just how that conversation would go. She truly hoped that Sebastian was coming to his senses and ready to somehow make up for his costly decisions of the past. At least when it came to her father. She was still unsure how to proceed with him when it came to her own feelings.

There was no denying the feelings that were still there. As infuriating as he was, and as upset as she was with him, Sebastian was still an alluring, compassionate man. He was a brilliant musician and composer. And there was no denying the natural ease and confidence she had witnessed when he had led the Symphony in LaPelle's absence. It was very appealing to say the least.

Penelope's thoughts were interrupted by a knock at her door. She untangled herself from the chair and went to look through the peep hole. What she saw surprised her and made her heart flutter for the second time that night. Outside stood an attendant behind a cart filled with the flowers from the dining room. She opened the door and greeted the young woman.

"Good evening, Ms. Dixon. I've been instructed to deliver these flowers to you. May I come in?"

"Yes, yes, please, come in." Penelope stepped aside allowing Anita, as her name tag read, push the cart into her room. "Please, just set them anywhere you can find room."

Anita proceeded to place the containers and vases on top of tables and even the dresser, filling nearly every inch of available surface.

"They're beautiful," Anita stated. "You must have quite the admirer."

"I suppose I do," Penelope returned quietly.

Once done, Anita said good night and left. Penelope returned to the center of the room and admired the lovely flowers. To see them fill her small area rather than spread throughout the larger meeting room filled her with awe. She gently fingered a few petals of a daffodil while she smelled the fragrant hyacinths. Looking around, she didn't notice the white tulip and supposed it had been beyond saving.

With nothing else in mind to do, she decided on going for a swim. She didn't think she'd have to worry about Sebastian making another surprise appearance, given that he was currently on the phone with her father. Although she didn't know how long the conversation would last, she still thought the last thing on Sebastian's mind would be getting in a workout.

Penelope grabbed another swimsuit from the dresser, and after changing, she made her way down to the pool.

She hoped a vigorous workout would clear her head and allow her a restful sleep tonight.

Chapter 15

Sebastian woke Wednesday morning in a better, more encouraging frame of mind. His talk with Bernard the night before went a long way in easing his guilt about taking their friendship for granted. He was aware that Bernard and Penelope had spoken just before he called, and Bernard was given the details of the how their evening went. Sebastian answered questions and filled in some of the blanks, and after apologizing to Bernard, he was reassured that their friendship was not in jeopardy. In fact, Bernard was all in favor of encouraging the reconciliation between Sebastian and Penelope.

That had certainly taken Sebastian by surprise. Bernard had said he was aware of the feelings they shared for one another, and even though their relationship took a bumpy detour, their reunion would be beautiful. He didn't go so far as to offer his help in any way at the moment, saying that he had meddled quite enough.

Bernard assured Sebastian that he would no doubt figure it out.

Sebastian went about his morning routine with his spirits high, focusing on positive thoughts about how the day would unfold. He had a quick cup of coffee in his room before deciding to leave early in order to get to Benaroya Hall, thinking he'd grab something more from Starbucks.

At ten after eight he was on his way, the vase of flowers in hand and his satchel containing LaPelle's notes and music slung over his shoulder. He had taken the time to retrieve them from LaPelle's office yesterday afternoon after his steamy yet disappointing encounter with Penelope.

Once he arrived, he quickly made his way to the recital hall, thankful that no one else was of a mind to go early. Placing the flowers on the piano brought a smile to his face, and he hoped that they'd do the same for Penelope. He then placed his coat over a chair and decided to head to Starbucks for more coffee and a scone.

As Sebastian approached the café, he saw Penelope and Lindsay sitting at a tall table, taking turns talking animatedly while sipping on iced drinks. Muffins sat untouched in front of them. He had no choice but to pass near them and as he did he offered a good morning.

Penelope hid her surprise and any animosity that may still be lingering from last night, and answered with a courteous hello. Lindsay said good morning as well, and Sebastian had the feeling she was fighting the urge to break out into a wide smile as her lips twitched with the beginnings of a grin.

He didn't linger for chit chat, but made his way to the counter to place his order. He remained there while his coffee was poured and the scone was bagged. Walking past the ladies again, he said he'd see them at rehearsal before making his way back to the recital hall.

Sebastian sat in a chair in the audience section finishing his coffee and scone as other members filed into the room. At a quarter till the hour, Penelope and Lindsay made their entrance. While Lindsay went to her section, Penelope approached the piano, pausing when she noticed the vase of flowers. And although she didn't look in Sebastian's direction, slightly disappointing him, she reached out to gently stroke the petals of the tulip.

His heart swelled as a smile took shape on Penelope's face.

Realizing it was time to get to it, he rose from the seat and took his spot behind the podium, making a few announcements before beginning the rehearsal. The next three hours went by quickly as Sebastian and the Symphony lost themselves in the music. His confidence had grown ten-fold since yesterday, and the unbelievable joy he felt at leading the orchestra was a welcomed emotion. At noon, he congratulated everyone on a terrific rehearsal and stated that he'd see everyone in the morning, same time as usual.

As the members began packing away their instruments and music, he watched Penelope and her interaction with some of the others. Her poise and grace, the ease with which she handled herself, were all fascinating. She had truly become an exquisite woman.

"A remarkable young woman, wouldn't you say?" Henry spoke softly from behind Sebastian.

Sebastian turned to face the man. "Yes. The Symphony is very fortunate to have her, as am I to have her play my composition."

"It will be a glorious series of performances." Changing the subject, Henry went on to inquire more about LaPelle.

"As I stated prior to beginning, he's taken a turn for the worse, I'm afraid. He has a respiratory infection, has lost his voice, and is being instructed to remain away from others for the next few days. He's on medications to aid in his recovery."

"Dreadful. I do hope he'll have a speedy one. But should it come to it, you leading us will be wonderful. We couldn't ask for a better substitute."

"Thank you for that, Henry."

Henry nodded his head and bid Sebastian a good afternoon.

"I'll see you tomorrow."

As the last of the musicians began to file out, Penelope and Lindsay lingered. He caught a glimpse of Penelope caressing the flowers once again. Just then, she happened to look his way and he offered her a genuine smile. He enjoyed seeing the blush across her cheeks before she turned away.

Even a millimeter is progress, said the snail.

Sebastian recalled that line from a children's story his mother used to recite to him.

Yes, even the smallest movement ahead is progress.

Sebastian gathered his items and made his way out of the room, a smile of his own lighting up his face.

—

Penelope shouldn't have let the flowers affect her so, but she couldn't help the smile that formed on her face when she first approached the piano. Sebastian had been thoughtful enough to place them, and he even managed to save the white tulip.

For your forgiveness.

His words came back to mind. One gesture wouldn't make up for all the hurt that had been caused, but it was a start.

"How easily we women can be swayed." Lindsay's teasing statement, along with the puppy-dog look in her eyes made Penelope chuckle.

"We're so weak when it comes to this mush, aren't we?" She teased right back.

"I think it's very sweet. At least he's trying."

Penelope gathered her items, following Lindsay out of the recital hall. "Yes, he is. We'll see where his persistency will lead."

They made their way onto University then up Sixth Avenue toward the Pacific Place complex.

"So you're going to give him a chance?" Lindsay asked expectantly.

"We'll see," Penelope answered with a mischievous smile.

"Of course you are. You're just not going to make it easy on him."

Penelope didn't answer as they dodged pedestrian traffic and vehicles, quickly making their way into the shopping complex. Once inside they took a moment to study the directory. "Anything in particular you feel like having for lunch? I'm thinking Pike Place Chowder sounds good."

"Penelope, you're avoiding my inquisition." Lindsay slipped off her coat and folded it over her satchel.

"Of course I'm not going to make it easy on him. Would you?" Penelope did the same with her coat and strode forward, intent on food.

"So you're going to torture the poor man, lead him on, dangle him on the line."

"I'm going to do no such thing. But I'm not going to just roll over and let him back in so easily. He has a lot to make up for, and if he's willing to prove that to me, well then, there just may be a chance for us."

"But you love him."

Penelope stopped and faced Lindsay. "Yes, I realized I do love him. Still. But there are years between us – and I'm not talking about our age. I'm talking about the time we've spent apart. We aren't the same people we were all those years ago. We have to reconnect with one another, and there must be honesty and trust first and foremost." She turned to resume walking.

"I understand. His sex appeal is only part of the equation."

Penelope swung her head around and found Lindsay grinning, causing her to burst out laughing. "Precisely," she sputtered.

Lindsay caught up with Penelope and looped their arms together as they continued walking. "It's good to see you loosening up, but you've got a ways to go."

"What do you mean?" Penelope asked.

"What I mean is that – and I say this with much love for my new friend – you're a young vibrant woman who at times acts much too..."

"*Too?*"

"How do I say this delicately? Too refined, cultured... stuffy?" She turned her scrunched up face to Penelope, causing her to chuckle.

"Is that so?"

"I'm not saying you have to go wild and lose *all* your inhibitions. Just relax more, stop taking everything so seriously, and enjoy life."

"I rather like the sound of that," Penelope admitted.

Lindsay stopped their progress and faced Penelope, pointing her finger at her like a mother teaching a lesson to a child. "See, that, that right there."

"What?" Penelope protested.

"I get that you're educated and proper and have manners to spare, but you sound like an English lady right out of "Downton Abbey".

"And that's a bad thing?" Penelope's look was one of true amusement.

"Not unless you're living in high society London."

"And this is '*Merica!*" she answered, attempting her best country accent.

"Right on." Lindsay laughed and once again looped their arms as they resumed the journey toward their destination.

Penelope thoroughly enjoyed the camaraderie she was developing with Lindsay, and for the next several hours, they were carefree as they ate lunch and shopped. That is, until they admitted they were tired of repeatedly undressing and dressing again, and decided to call it a day.

Yet they did it all over again the following afternoon, finding

Keyed Up

several new outfits and ordering gowns from Nordstrom for the upcoming performances. Penelope informed Lindsay about the spa session she had planned for them Friday afternoon, and both voiced how eager and excited they were. After a rough start to her week, Penelope had enjoyed some sense of routine for a few days which included a swim every evening and no eventful encounters with Sebastian.

The morning rehearsals were the only interaction she'd had with him. And although he didn't make an attempt to seek her out afterwards, nor did she run across him in the Fairmont, he did manage to make sure she knew he was thinking of her.

When Penelope arrived for rehearsal Thursday morning, going straight to Starbucks for her favorite Frappuccino, she was told that she didn't have to pay because her purchase was already taken care of. When her order was ready and she reached for her cup, instead of her name on the side, there was a drawing of a daffodil. And Friday morning, she was surprised by room service as a waiter brought in a tray of food with a single red rose lying in the middle.

Penelope was delighted with Sebastian's sweet gestures and couldn't help but wonder what other surprises he had in store. She also couldn't help but think she felt like a pushover for finding such joy in his attempts.

Was she being shallow? Easily swayed? Were his actions simple ploys, or were they sincere and meant to assure her of his want for her?

Whatever the case, she told herself that she'd be cautious, keep an open mind, and try to spare her heart any more misery.

Not too much to ask for, right?

Chapter 16

As Friday's rehearsal began to wrap up, Sebastian made the rounds throughout each section of the orchestra to ascertain if there were any concerns regarding the selections, and to get an idea of who would be attending the reception at Tulio's later that evening. He wanted to make a personable connection with as many of the members as he could to show them he was approachable.

After a few pointers here and light conversation there, he went to Penelope as she was pulling the cover down over the keys on the piano. When she turned his way, he gave her a friendly nod.

"I have to say," Sebastian started, "if our performance was tomorrow, the orchestra would be more than ready."

"Yes, everyone sounds magnificent," she agreed with a smile. "And you're doing exceptionally well as the director."

"Thank you for that, Penelope. I wanted to ask, since I believe Ms. Beacham emailed us separately, what did you think of her article? It should be online already, but I didn't take the time to check this morning."

As Penelope started to put on her coat, Sebastian was quick to offer assistance, lifting one side as she slipped her arm in. She turned to thank him, her words barely a whisper as they came face to face.

"You're welcome." He let his eyes roam from hers, down to her lips and back again. She didn't look away, but steadily held his gaze. How Sebastian wanted to taste her; wrap her up and steal her away to someplace much more private.

Penelope took a half step back. "I thought her article was perfect and told her so. I didn't think anything needed revising. As for checking online, I didn't take the time to look this morning either. I was too busy enjoying breakfast in my room. Thank you for that, by the way."

Sebastian smiled, delighted. "You're very welcome. I hope you enjoyed it. I would've liked to have joined you, but thought it may be too soon."

"Perhaps." She smiled coyly. "Have you been taking the time to enjoy any of Seattle?" she asked, changing the subject.

"Not really. I did take time, however to go shopping for a suit, and I ordered a tuxedo, should I find myself fulfilling the duty of Maestro when opening night arrives. How about you?"

"I have. Lindsay and I have done a great deal of shopping ourselves and the break in the rain has been nice. It's allowed us to enjoy walking around the city. I haven't made it to Pike Place Market, but that's on the list." She strung her satchel over her shoulder as she flashed him a brilliant smile.

"Are you free this afternoon? Maybe I could show you around the Market."

She bowed her head briefly then returned his gaze. "I'm afraid I can't. I have more plans with Lindsay, and then I'll be getting ready for this evening."

"Well, I'll let you get to it and I'll see you this evening at seven."

"Yes. Have a good afternoon."

"You, too, Penelope."

They stood staring at one another, neither moving, neither blinking. There were so many things he wanted to blurt out, but knew it wasn't the time, and certainly not the place. He hoped for at least a few moments alone with Penelope this evening, because while doing the little bit of shopping he did for himself, he had also purchased a gift for her that he hoped she would accept.

Sebastian was about to ask if he could escort her to Tulio's this evening when Lindsay stepped to Penelope's side.

"Ready for lunch and some pampering?"

Penelope quickly turned her way as she was brought out of her daze. "Yes, absolutely." She turned back to Sebastian. "See you tonight."

"Yes you will." He bowed his head to the ladies and turned to leave. At some point he would monopolize a few moments of her time. Until then, he'd have a light lunch and get in a trip to the gym this afternoon.

He realized it'd only been a few days, but his interaction with Penelope had certainly turned around in that short time, giving him hope. He wanted nothing more than for it to continue on its promising course. Sebastian told himself to remain steadfast and not get overzealous, chancing any set back.

Patience and balance were becoming his new mantra.

—

"I wasn't sure if I should have given you another minute, or if you were in need of rescuing," Lindsay said.

Penelope watched Sebastian exit the room before she turned to her friend. "Neither, really. Sebastian was asking me if I would like to go to Pike Place Market, but I told him you and I had plans."

"Oh, well darn that you have to miss out on a date with him," Lindsay quipped.

"Don't be silly. It wouldn't have been a date."

"Well, double-darn." She grinned.

"Lindsay, if it weren't for the spa, you would've come up with an excuse to bail on me, wouldn't you?"

"Possibly. Maybe you *should* consider a date with Sebastian though. Or invite him to join us at The Triple Door Lounge tonight after Tulio's."

Penelope thought about that for a moment, thinking it wouldn't be such a bad idea. "I'll think about it," she said, not sure why she wasn't ready to let on that she'd actually really like that.

"You do that."

They made their way back to the Fairmont for a light lunch and three hours of decadent treatment at the spa.

Once they parted ways, Penelope took a nap, feeling wonderfully relaxed after the massage and facial. She woke at five-thirty, leaving plenty of time to get ready. After snacking on a banana and a granola bar, she took a shower, did her hair and make-up, and slipped on her new black Kassidy Lace dress from Francesca's that stopped mid-thigh. She then put on black sheer stockings and knee-high suede wedge boots. Silver hoop earrings completed her outfit.

She was excited for the evening, and couldn't help but wonder what Sebastian would think of her appearance.

Turned out that she wouldn't have to wait too long to find out the answer.

At six-thirty, a knock sounded at her door. When she looked through the peep hole, she was amused to see Sebastian there, as if her thoughts had conjured him. Admittedly, she was a bit anxious as well.

Penelope opened the door and was elated to see the instant look of appreciation and desire on his face as his gaze slowly scanned her from head to toe and back again. She too, did her share of admiring, thinking how amazing he looked in his silver-gray wool suit with mint green shirt and pewter tie.

"You take my breath away," Sebastian said.

Penelope knew she was blushing as she felt the rush of heat across her entire body. *Oh how this man affects me. There is no resisting him.*

"I know this is presumptuous of me, but I had hoped to escort you to Tulio's."

"Oh, all right. Please, come in." She stepped back to allow his entry.

"Thank you." As Sebastian walked past her into the room, she was surrounded by his intoxicating scent. Whatever cologne he had on was more than enticing. It made her want to snuggle up to him for the entire night. And wasn't that a dangerous thought?

"Let me just get my purse and I'll be ready." Penelope walked to her dresser, placing a few items in a small silver clutch. Satisfied with what she thought she'd need, she turned back toward Sebastian.

And stopped in her tracks.

His look of longing, of sexual hunger made her knees weak. There was no mistaking his desire. And she could no longer deny her desire for him.

"Penelope, you are the most beautiful woman in the world." When she began to deny his claim, he stopped her as he took a step closer. "Please, let me say this while I still have my wits about me, and while I have this moment with you." He took another step, bringing them within arms' reach of one another. "I know it's only been a few days, and while I promised I'd give you time and space, it's been torture to hardly speak to you, to not touch you. I've wanted to make up for lost time and spend every waking moment with you."

"Oh, Sebastian." Slowly she began to let her walls crumble.

He stepped within inches of her and she could feel his heat surround her, engulf her. Set her ablaze.

"I said I'd do my best not to push, and I'll continue to try, but I will constantly remind you of my presence." His half smile was so roguishly handsome she nearly gave in to the craving of wanting to taste his lips. She watched him slip his hand into his coat pocket, pulling out a blue box. "I'd be honored if you'd accept this gift from me. A small token of my love and what you mean to me."

Without giving her time to respond, he opened the box and withdrew a silver chain. At the end of the chain was a silver heart key pendant. It sparkled beautifully as it swung from his hand. He set the box aside and palmed the pendant, showing her the diamond that was centered in the heart.

"It's gorgeous! But Sebastian—"

"But nothing." He stepped to her backside, draping the necklace around her. "Penelope, you mean the world to me, and I'm only sorry it took so long for me to realize. This is a small symbol of my love. This may sound very cheesy, but you hold the key to my heart." Once he had it clasped, his hands lingered on her shoulders and he placed a tender kiss at the nape of her neck.

Penelope fingered the pendant and shuddered at Sebastian's touch. Turning in his arms, they shared a mutual look of want as his hands found her waist and brought her body flush with his. Dropping her purse from her hand, she looped both around his neck as his mouth descended on hers for a breath-stealing kiss that she returned with just as much passion. Their hunger had them practically devouring one another as needy moans escaped them both.

When Sebastian broke from the kiss, Penelope didn't hesitate to frame his face and pull him back in for more. She didn't want this wondrous feeling they were cocooned in to end, but Sebastian broke away again to rest his forehead against hers.

"As much as I'd like to take this further, if we don't stop, we'll never leave this room tonight. And I don't think you're quite ready for that. Besides," he eyed her body again, "you look too gorgeous not to go show off."

All Penelope could do was laugh and nod her head at first until she found her voice. She stepped out of his embrace, saying, "I'll be right back." Walking to the bathroom, she was glad her legs didn't give way, as weak as they felt. *That man can kiss!* She fluffed her hair then reapplied her lipstick. Fingering the necklace again, she thought how perfectly beautiful it was and what it symbolized from Sebastian. She had to stop herself from getting misty-eyed which would further delay them if her eye make-up ran. Chuckling at herself, she rejoined Sebastian.

He had his coat draped across one arm as his other held her purse which he had retrieved from the floor. She pulled her coat out of the closet and accepted her clutch from Sebastian.

"Ready," she said.

Sebastian led the way to the door, opening it for her to exit first. He closed the door and escorted her to the elevator. Once inside, they rode in silence, exchanging timid glances and silly grins. When they reached the lobby, Sebastian helped her into her coat before putting his on and leading her out the doors. He linked his hand with hers, sending a thrill through her. The restaurant was only two blocks away, so their walk would be quick.

Penelope felt as if she were on her first date with him. She felt as if the time was right for a fresh start, given that they'd already let too much time slip through their fingers.

"Sebastian," she began, "Lindsay and I were planning on going to The Triple Door Lounge after Tulio's. There's a singer I met at the Fairmont, Cheryl, the hostess at Shucker's. She and her group, Euphoria will be performing there tonight. Would you care to join us?"

"I'd like that very much, thank you." He turned to her and said, "I'm beginning to rethink showing you off tonight. You do realize I'm going to have a hard time watching other men lay eyes on you? You look truly stunning and will no doubt grab everyone's attention."

"Thank you, Sebastian, but I couldn't care less about anyone else besides you laying eyes on me." She knew her statement was bold, but also knew that's what Sebastian was waiting for; for her to make the next move. It felt good to take initiative. Perhaps she was finding her confidence after all.

They were approaching their destination, and before Penelope could take another step, Sebastian had her in his arms and was once again kissing her senseless. She paid no attention to their surroundings or any others nearby; no doubt some of them members of the orchestra who were bound to recognize the two of them. As quickly as the kiss had started, Sebastian pulled away, brushing his thumb beneath her bottom lip.

"You'll have to fix your lipstick again." He winked.

"Rascal," she countered before laughing.

He took her hand and led her inside where they were escorted to a private dining room reserved for the reception. Dozens of people were already milling about and the soft buzz of conversation filled the room. When their coats were checked, Sebastian linked hands with her as they began to make the rounds.

Chapter 17

Sebastian couldn't have been happier accompanying Penelope. The atmosphere was relaxed as they were introduced to members of the Symphony Board and Foundation, and visited with the musicians. He was pleased with himself at how easily he blended and conversed with everyone, thinking it was beyond time for him to pull himself out of his self-imposed reclusive life. Penelope certainly helped with that, easily socializing with everyone and making him feel at ease; making him feel included.

Sebastian was even more pleased to have the acceptance of the Symphony with him as Interim Conductor until LaPelle was able to resume his duties.

After exchanging daily emails with LaPelle, he had been able to keep him abreast as to how the rehearsals were going. Every day LaPelle expressed his regret for not getting better; as if he had control over such things. His condition had been improving, but certainly not as quickly as he would've liked. Sebastian assured him that he would eventually be well again, that he needed to take it easy, and to allow his body to take care of itself.

Penelope, of course, was as gracious as ever and was certainly winning over every person she met. She was articulate and out-going, and gave attention to anyone who approached her. She even sought out those who seemed to be too timid to approach her on their own. A short time later, Lindsay arrived and they were inseparable.

Lindsay looked nearly as stunning in a dark blue, loose fitting dress. Her auburn hair was piled on her head with loose curls framing her face. She and Penelope were attracting attention from many in the room.

After offering the ladies a glass of wine, Sebastian excused himself to use the restroom. As he exited, about to round the corner, he stopped short when he heard two male voices. One of them mentioned Penelope's name in his slurred speech.

"That Penelope Dixon is quite a piece. Lucky to have landed this position. I know she's got talent, I've seen her perform, but I'm sure it doesn't hurt who her father is and now she's in bed with Sebastian Mauer."

"That's uncalled for," another voice stated. "You don't know that."

"Don't you think so? Look at them together and tell me he's not getting a piece of that?"

The second man made a sound of disgust. "That's–"

"That's highly inappropriate talk," Sebastian stated, surprising the men as he approached.

"Ah, there's the hero," said the man who'd obviously already had too much to drink. He was a stocky man, probably near fifty, and although tastefully dressed, his manners were that of a rube. His drink sloshed out of his glass and onto his hands as he staggered toward Sebastian.

Sebastian noticed that the other man grimaced, as if embarrassed for his companion. He was tall and lean, also smartly dressed. He reached for his friend before he could make contact with Sebastian.

"Uh, Mr. Mauer, I'm William Stone, and this intoxicated man is my brother-in-law, Gary Brown." He was clearly annoyed with his relative. "I apologize for his comments, they're–"

"Oh, don't go apologizing for me, *Mr. Stone*," he said. "We men can talk, can't we Sebastian?" He managed to slap his hand down on Sebastian's shoulder as if they were chums.

Sebastian merely looked at the man and managed to remove his hand without wrenching it behind his back as he would've liked. William took Gary by the shoulders and once again tried to rein him in.

"As happily married as I am, and don't tell Cecelia this, *Billy*," he said to William, "but I can't help but picture what a young, luscious body that Penelope is hiding underneath that little dress. But you must know, am I right?"

His laughter that rang out was short-lived as Sebastian punched him in the mouth and sent him crashing to the floor. William wisely stood by not saying a word or offering help to Gary, who moaned as he squirmed, trying to roll himself over.

"Sebastian!"

He turned to see that a group of people had gathered behind him, including Penelope and Lindsay. He took a step away from the men as Penelope ran to his side. She lifted his right hand, examining the redness that was already spreading across his knuckles.

"What was that for?" Her look of worry and near horror wasn't what Sebastian wanted to see mar her beautiful face.

But before Sebastian could answer, William spoke up. "For defending your honor against my drunken, foul-mouthed brother-in-law."

"I don't understand? What's going on?"

Another gentleman entered the scene, Sebastian recognizing him as the president of the foundation board, Mr. Heitz. "William, care to explain?"

"Unfortunately Gary had too much to drink, and although that's no excuse, he thought he could discuss Ms. Dixon with Mr. Mauer in a very unflattering way." He turned to Sebastian and Penelope, and continued. "Again, I apologize for his comments and behavior. He had no right to say or do such things. Never again will I give in to my sister's pleas of bringing him along."

"Thank you for the apology," Sebastian said. "I don't normally condone actions such as that, and I would apologize for *my* behavior, but it felt much too satisfying."

"That's quite all right. I'm going to escort him home and ensure that he never steps foot near either of you, nor inside Benaroya Hall again." William leaned down, and with the aid of another, they hoisted Gary onto his feet and practically dragged him toward the exit.

Mr. Heitz addressed the crowd. "Well, that's enough excitement for one evening." He chuckled nervously. "Let's all return to the dining room and continue to enjoy ourselves. Mr. Mauer, Ms. Dixon, I hope you'll stay and continue to mingle with the others. I do apologize for the disruption."

"Thank you, sir," Penelope said. "It was not of your doing. We'll be along shortly."

As the crowd dispersed, Penelope remained at Sebastian's side while Lindsay stood nearby.

"Sebastian, you should get some ice for your hand. At the very least, go into the bathroom and wash it under cold water." She tenderly ran her fingers along the tops of his knuckles.

"I'll do that. I'm sorry you had to witness that. Not one of my finer moments, but I'd do it again in a heartbeat if anyone ever insults you again."

"Very chivalrous of you," Lindsay commented, earning smiles.

"Thank you for standing up for me, although shutting him down with words would've been more ideal."

"Yes, well, a good punch was much more quick and effective. Not to mention, gratifying."

Lindsay giggled then tried to put on a straight face. "I'll leave you two alone. See you back in there," she nodded to the private room before heading off.

Sebastian looked at Penelope and gently stroked her cheek with his uninjured hand. "That man was crass and I'm sorry if you heard his words. I'm sorry-"

"Stop." She placed a tender kiss to his lips. "You don't have to be sorry for another person's ignorant behavior. He doesn't know us. He hasn't the first clue about our relationship, so his words mean nothing to me."

"Gracious as ever."

"Hmm. Get into the bathroom and wash." She nudged him in that direction.

"Care to join me? I may need your assistance." He winked and grinned wickedly.

Penelope's laughter was a sweet sound to Sebastian. "I think you can handle it. I'll be inside with Lindsay."

Before she could walk away, Sebastian gathered her close for another kiss. He loved seeing her smile when he released her. "I won't be long."

"See that you aren't." Sebastian watched her turn and walk back to the reception. He then went to the bathroom to make quick work of washing his hand. Far be it from him to keep the lady waiting.

—

Penelope was immediately surrounded by several of the Symphony members, including Lindsay and Henry.

"My dear, is everything all right?" Henry asked.

"It is now, thank you, Henry. One of the guests got a bit carried away and had to be–"

"Carried away," Lindsay offered. "Unbelievable," she shook her head. "Here." She handed Penelope a glass of wine.

"Thank you, Lindsay. It's been taken care of, so let's put it behind us and enjoy ourselves."

"Indeed," Henry added. "It's been a pleasant gathering, so let's not let anything else spoil it."

As the voices chattered around her, Penelope kept her eyes on the door, awaiting Sebastian's return. In the next instant, the door opened and there he was. She immediately felt her lips curve upwards in a smile and she couldn't look away. And why would she want to? He was the most handsome, intriguing man, and he could be hers. He made it known that he *was* hers. She reached for the necklace as his words from when he had presented it to her came back to mind.

You hold the key to my heart.

"I meant to tell you how beautiful that necklace is and how lovely it looks on you." Lindsay spoke softly at Penelope's side. "A gift from Sebastian?"

"Yes," Penelope answered as she watched the man in question make his way across the room, stopping briefly to speak with those who got his attention.

"A Tiffany pendant. That's almost the equivalent of an engagement ring." When Penelope turned to Lindsay, she continued. "You don't look shocked or frightened. That's good, right? The man loves you, and you've told me you love him. Don't fight it, Penelope."

"I realize there is no fighting it, Lindsay."

"I'm glad to hear it, and I'm sure he will be too." As Sebastian came closer, Lindsay excused herself to go speak with other members.

Before Penelope allowed her to step away, she gave her a quick hug. "You've become a dear friend." When Penelope pulled away, she added, "And I don't think I've told you how beautiful you look. That dress was the perfect choice."

"Thanks." Lindsay blushed at Penelope before walking away just as Sebastian reached her side.

"You and Lindsay have become quite close in such a short time."

"Yes," she stated as she watched Lindsay join another group. "And I'm very thankful for that. She's a wonderful person." She turned back towards Sebastian, completely comfortable with his nearness. "Hand feeling better?" She brought his hand up to inspect it, and was glad to see that the redness and swelling were minimal.

"Never felt better." Sebastian teased as his other hand played with a few curls around her face. "You don't seem to mind our display of... closeness."

She tipped her face to his, staring into the depths of his sea green eyes. They seemed to darken the longer she gazed at them and little lines fanned out from the corners as a smile brightened his face. With their hands joined, her other went to his shoulder, being careful not to spill the wine she still held. Sebastian brought his free hand around her back, pulling her close as they swayed in time to the soft music that filled the room.

"I rather like our closeness." She rested her head on his shoulder as he set a smooth rhythm to which they moved. They stayed in each other's arms for what seemed like hours.

Reluctantly, they were drawn out of their embrace when Mr. Heitz and another board member approached.

"Mr. Mauer, Ms. Dixon," he began. "This is Ms. Gordon, one of the orchestra representatives. We were very pleased with the article you two consented to with Ms. Kimberly Beacham. We read it online this afternoon and it was excellent. Congratulations to both of you, and most importantly, a thank you. Your presence with the Symphony is a great boon; one that will hopefully close out the remainder of the season with a flourish."

Penelope spoke first, offering her thanks for the wonderful opportunity. "In such a short time I've come to really enjoy Seattle, and the members of the orchestra have been most welcoming."

"It's been an honor to work with the Symphony," Sebastian added. "Having Penelope debut my piece is a dream come true. The unexpected surprise of taking over as the director has been enlightening and exhilarating."

"We're of course wishing LaPelle a speedy recovery," Ms. Gordon said. "But it's my understanding that you're fully prepared to conduct the Symphony should LaPelle be unable to do so."

Penelope admired Sebastian as he effortlessly conversed with the board members. He was never meant to hide himself away from the public. He was meant to shine. His multiple talents of performing, composing, and now conducting were a true gift; ones that should grace the world.

As she continued to think on that, a proud smile garnishing her face, Sebastian gave her a curious look as he finished talking before Heitz and Gordon walked away.

"What is that coy smile for?"

"You. All my smiles are for you." She wrapped her arm around his waist as she now led him around the room to visit with others.

As the evening wore on and it approached eight-thirty, most of the guests had already said good night. Penelope caught up with Lindsay and asked if she was ready to go to the lounge to see Euphoria.

"Most definitely."

"I thought so. I called a cab to come pick us up. It should be here any moment. Sebastian's getting our coats."

Penelope linked arms with Lindsay as they went out front to meet up with Sebastian.

"Cab's here," he said as he helped the ladies with their coats. They climbed in the cab, ready for the next phase of their evening's entertainment.

Chapter 18

The three arrived at the Lounge before it got too crowded. Once inside, they were immediately escorted to a booth against the wall, close to the stage.

"Cheryl insisted," the hostess explained with a smile. "I'll leave our drink menu and be right back with some water.

"Wow, we get the five star treatment," Lindsay said as she sat on one end of the half-moon booth. Penelope sat in the middle while Sebastian took the other end.

"That's very nice of Cheryl to reserve a booth for us," Penelope added. At that moment, she saw Cheryl headed their way.

She smiled radiantly as she said hello to everyone. Dressed in a violet vintage sleeveless dress with flared skirt, Cheryl exuded style and sex appeal; much like the women of the Ginger Rogers and Rita Hayworth era. Her hair was styled smoothly as it hung down to her shoulders, a slight under-curl at the end. One side was pulled back with a diamond clip.

"So glad you could all make it," Cheryl said in greeting.

"Love your dress." Lindsay complimented.

"Thanks. Gotta love DressLily."

"Right?" Lindsay grinned.

"We're excited to see you and your group perform. Cheryl, let me introduce you to Lindsay Clarke, flautist with the Symphony, and my friend. And this is Sebastian Mauer, as I know you're aware; performer, composer, and more recently, conductor."

Cheryl shook hands with both. "Really? What happened with LaPelle?"

"Cheryl follows the Symphony, and since the website hasn't officially announced Sebastian's interim role–"

"Of course you'd be curious," Sebastian added. "He unfortunately became ill and is still trying to recover. He hopes to be back for the performances."

"But Sebastian is prepared," Penelope started, "and more than capable of conducting us, should it come to that."

"I see. How wonderful. Kimberly Beacham's article with Seattle Magazine was terrific. There was a link to it on the Symphony's website."

"The wonders of technology and social media," Sebastian quipped.

"There's no escaping it." Cheryl chuckled. "Care to have some drinks? Their selection is tremendous." At that moment, the waitress returned with glasses and carafe of water.

"I'll have whatever Riesling you recommend," Penelope ordered.

"And I'd like the Chartreuse, please," Lindsay ordered next.

"I'll have a glass of the Dewars," Sebastian finished.

"Excellent, I'll be back shortly." The waitress nodded.

The members of Euphoria began to gather on stage and prepare for their show. The group consisted of a pianist, a drummer, a stand-up bass player, and a guitarist.

"Mmm, who's the guitarist?" Lindsay asked as her eyes stayed locked on the handsome man.

"That's Kellen," Cheryl answered. "And he's currently available," she added with a sly grin.

"Well, now," Lindsay drawled, earning quiet laughter from everyone. Lindsay turned back to the group. "What? I can look, right?"

"You absolutely can," Cheryl added. "I better go, we're about to start. Hope you all enjoy the show and I'll be back when we take a break."

"I'm sure we will. Have fun," Penelope cheered.

As Cheryl made her way toward her bandmates, the lights around the lounge began to dim as the stage lit up. Applause rang out as the singer stepped up to the microphone.

"Thank you, and welcome, to the Triple Door Lounge. I'm Cheryl, and we are Euphoria." She swept her hand from one end of the stage to the other as each member bowed their heads. The pianist started, followed by the drummer, and one by one each musician began, leading into their first song, "The Look of Love" by Diana Krall.

For the next forty-five minutes, the band ran through a medley of songs and styles, ranging from Norah Jones and Alicia Keys to Nat King Cole and Frank Sinatra. They also mixed in a few original pieces of their own, which Penelope thoroughly enjoyed. Just before their break, Cheryl made an announcement.

"Thank you for coming out tonight, folks. There's plenty more to follow. I wanted to welcome some special guests who are here tonight, members of the Seattle Symphony. Lindsay Clarke, Penelope Dixon, and Sebastian Mauer!"

As applause rang out and a spot light focused briefly on the three of them, they raised their hands to wave to the crowd.

"They've got a fantastic series of performances lined up, so if you haven't already, be sure to get your tickets!" With that, Cheryl exited the stage as the house lights brightened and the rest of Euphoria followed her, making their way to her guests.

"Oh, crud, I haven't even had time to powder the shine off my face," Lindsay said as she rummaged through her purse.

"Lindsay, you look beautiful." Penelope placed her hand on Lindsay's, stilling her movements.

"She's right," Sebastian added. "Any man would be honored to make your acquaintance."

"Thank you, guys." Her cheeks blushed and she glowed, enhancing her lovely appearance and negating the need for any further make-up.

Cheryl and the band arrived at the booth and introductions were made. After a moment of greetings and praises from all parties, most of the guys made excuses to use the facilities and grab a drink. Kellen asked if he could join them and offered to buy Lindsay another drink.

"Y-yes. Thank you," Lindsay said. Before long, the waitress brought her another Chartreuse.

Sebastian scooted closer to Penelope, inviting Cheryl to have a seat.

"Thanks for the spotlight," Penelope said, a teasing tone in her voice.

"Well, you know, we artists have to look out for one another. So," she started again, looking back and forth between Penelope and Sebastian, "can I assume that the two of you are reunited?"

Penelope noticed Sebastian raise an eyebrow at her while giving his devilish half-smile. Instinctively, her hand went to the pendant as it had been doing most of the evening. "You could say that," Penelope replied. "After all, who could resist this?" She palmed his cheek before raking her fingers across his whiskers as their gazes locked on one another.

"I'd resist all but you," he whispered against her lips before giving her a soft kiss.

"And that answers that." Cheryl laughed. "You look so happy. I'm glad for you both."

Penelope and Sebastian nodded simultaneously while they continued to exchange silly grins. After small conversation, Cheryl excused herself to freshen up. When the lights began to dim again, Kellen, reluctantly it seemed, left Lindsay's side to return to the stage.

Lindsay slid close to Penelope, grabbing her arm and giggling. "He asked me out!" she whisper-shouted.

"That's terrific."

"I know!" Lindsay threw back the rest of her drink before taking a sip of water. "Okay, bathroom break."

"Agreed," Penelope said. "I can't believe I haven't gone since I left the Fairmont." She turned to Sebastian and told him they'd be right back. The ladies scrambled out of the booth as Cheryl began singing "When Will I See You Again" by the Three Degrees.

Arm in arm they walked to the restroom, both floating as if on cloud nine.

"So," Lindsay began, "are you and Sebastian going to call it an early night and head back to the Fairmont?" She wiggled her eyebrows suggestively.

"I haven't really given it any thought," she fibbed.

"What?" Lindsay gave her the most perplexed look. "As close as you two have been tonight and you all but confirming that you're back together; and you don't want some alone time together?"

Penelope didn't answer as they entered the restroom, each of them taking care of business. As they met at the sink and washed their hands, Lindsay stared at Penelope.

"Because it wouldn't hurt my feelings if you wanted to leave at any time. I mean, I'm having a grand time, but if you and Sebastian, you know, want to be *alone,* I would completely understand. I'll arrange for a cab to take me home."

Again, Penelope remained quiet, pensive.

"Penelope, what's wrong?"

Penelope looked at Lindsay as she turned to her, a concerned look on her face. "I've dreamed about being alone with Sebastian for years, and now that I think it may come to that – as you would say – I'm completely freaking out."

"Why? Because it's been a while? You're rediscovering one another. Are you afraid you'll compare him to others or he'll do the same? How long has it been since you've been with someone?"

"Never," she said softly.

Lindsay stared wide-eyed and open-mouthed at her before asking, "Come again?"

Penelope closed her eyes and took a deep breath before answering. When she looked again to Lindsay, she tried hard to keep her nerves under control. "I've never been with Sebastian, or anyone else for that matter."

"You're a virgin." She looked at Penelope, clearly astonished. When Penelope only nodded her head, Lindsay continued. "That's amazing actually. I mean not that that's anything to be ashamed of. Did you actually wait for Sebastian?"

"Not intentionally. When we were together, I loved him so much and thought he'd be my first. When that didn't happen, I never dated or got close to anyone. Certainly no one I wanted to be intimate with. Even now, I can't imagine being with anyone but Sebastian." Penelope twisted her hands together, feeling ridiculous. "You probably think that's pathetic."

"Oh my God, no! I think that's the most romantic thing I've ever heard. And here you are, finally reunited."

"I'm ready to have him back in my life, ready for us to try again, but I'm scared as well."

"Scared? Why?" Lindsay rested her hands on Penelope's arms.

"What if I disappoint him? What if I'm not what he wants, physically, after all?"

"Are you kidding? Have you not seen the way that man looks at you? He worships you. You could never disappoint him. I think the best thing you can do is talk to him. Be open and honest."

When Penelope dipped her head again, Lindsay lifted her chin, making eye contact. "In case you didn't know, he loves you." She grinned.

Penelope smiled, trying to stifle a laugh. "I may have an inkling."

"Then go, be with him, talk to him, love him."

Penelope pulled Lindsay in for a hug. When they separated, Penelope had to wipe a tear from her eye. "Are you sure you don't want us to see you home?"

"Hey, I'm a big girl. Thank you, but no. I don't plan on having anymore to drink except water. I'll call a cab and be fine."

"All right. Thank you, Lindsay."

"Always so proper." She laughed. "You're welcome. Let's go."

Before they made it out the door, Penelope stopped, pulling her phone out of her purse. "I might as well call a cab for us right now."

"Atta girl."

Once the call was complete, they returned to their booth to find Sebastian with a worried look on his face.

"Everything all right?"

"Perfect," Penelope answered as Lindsay sat at the opposite end of the booth. When Sebastian moved to allow her to sit, she stopped him. "Actually, we're leaving."

"We are?" He looked from Penelope to Lindsay and back again. "Are you sure everything's all right?"

"Absolutely," Lindsay chimed in. "You kids go on, I'm going to stay for a while and then call a cab." She made a shooing motion as she said, "Go on now. Have a good evening." She grinned at Penelope and gave her a wink.

"Please tell Cheryl we'll return another night." She would've waved to her, being as they were so close to the stage, but she didn't want to distract her. "Good night, Lindsay."

"Will do. Good night."

Penelope linked arms with Sebastian, leading him through the lounge and outside to an awaiting cab.

"Penelope, what's going on?" he asked once they were settled in back.

His only answer was a stirring kiss.

Chapter 19

Sebastian was so caught up in Penelope's kiss that he almost forgot he'd asked a question. When she broke the kiss, she answered, "We'll talk when we get back to my room."

He simply nodded and pulled her close. Thankfully, the ride had been quick, and within moments they were pulling into the motorcoach entrance. Sebastian was thankful for the cover as it started raining. After paying for the ride and entering the lobby, he and Penelope remained quiet as they rode the elevator up to her room.

Penelope led the way down the hall. When they reached her door, she used her key card and pushed her way inside. Sebastian followed, curious as to what was going on with her. She shed her coat and hung it up, inviting Sebastian to remove his. When he did and handed it to her, she hung it in the closet as well.

Sebastian watched her, hoping she was ready to explain. Without saying a word, she stepped to him and slid her hands up the front of his coat, linking them behind his neck. With her boots on, they were practically eye to eye. She kept her gaze on him as she leaned in, taking his mouth in a slow, seductive kiss. When she broke the kiss and licked her lips, it was all Sebastian could do to hold back and not ravage her mouth.

"While you won't find me complaining about you kissing me as often as you'd like, what was that all about?"

"You may have gathered that I'm ready to let you back in. I can't deny my love for you, and I want us to start over again, Sebastian."

He saw the truth in her eyes and couldn't have been more elated.

He rested his forehead on hers and closed his eyes, letting her words sink in. "I can't tell you how happy that makes me."

"Oh, I think I can," she whispered as she crushed her body to his, no doubt feeling his erection pressing into her lower abdomen.

Sebastian held her tight as he took the initiative to ravage her mouth as he'd longed to do all night. His hands slid down her back to cup her rear, pulling her as close as he could. When she moaned into his mouth he continued his assault, stroking her with his tongue, nipping her with his teeth.

He broke away to nibble her neck and brought his hands up to find the zipper at the back of her dress. When he started to pull it down, she pulled away.

"Sebastian, I need to talk to you first." Her look of worry halted his actions. He watched Penelope step away and pull her lip in between her teeth, her brow furrowing. When she sat on the edge of the bed, he kept his distance, wanting her to feel comfortable with anything she had to say.

"I really don't know how to say this." She managed a half-hearted laugh before continuing, "except to just say it." She met his gaze, and he thought he saw actual terror in her blue eyes.

Her look of uncertainty compelled him to sit at her side and take her hands in his. "What is it? You can tell me."

"More than anything I want to be with you, but I, I've never been with anyone before, and I don't want to disappoint you."

Sebastian was in awe of her confession and wanted to ease any fears she had. "Penelope, I love you with all my heart, and God willing, I will love you tenderly with my body as well. I'm humbled and honored. I want to be your first and *only* love."

"I want that too. I've waited so long for you."

"You, you waited, for me?"

"Admittedly, not intentionally. After we first met and I realized that I loved you, I thought you *would* be my first and only. But when we, you–"

"When I pushed you away." He finished for her, distaste filling his mouth.

"Afterwards, I never got close to anyone. I never felt I could love anyone as I did you; as I still do. I'm so sorry I couldn't admit that sooner."

"Don't," he shook his head at her. "Don't ever be sorry. I'm the one who owes you more than a mere apology could ever rectify. I pushed you away, then sent you mixed signals, confusing you even more with what I see now as ridiculous reasons. Can you ever forgive me?"

"I already have. I want to move on from the past and build our future together; whatever that may entail, wherever that may lead."

"I want that too. I want *you*. It doesn't matter where we are or what we–"

"Do? So now you're going to regale me with your poetry?" She grinned.

Sebastian laughed, pulling her in for a hug. "I will regale you with whatever you want to hear."

Penelope pulled from his embrace. "Then tell me you'll make love to me."

He met her gaze and poured all his emotions into his words. "Nothing would please me more than to make love to you." Before he could say another word, Penelope stood and turned around, offering her back to him so that he could finish unzipping her dress. Sebastian stood and placed his hands on her shoulders. He brushed aside her hair and kissed her bare skin, enjoying the shudder he felt from her. "But Penelope, I have no protection with me." As much as he hated to stall their momentum, they had to be concerned with protection.

Penelope's next words couldn't have been more shocking. She tipped her face up to look over her shoulder at him. "I trust you. I never plan to be with anyone else, and if our night together results in a pregnancy, then nothing would make me happier."

Sebastian stepped around her, holding her arms. "Penelope, think about what you're saying."

"Do you not want children?" She looked hurt, disappointed.

"I never thought of having children when you were no longer in my life, to be honest. Don't you think the subject should have a bit more discussion?"

After a moment of silence, she continued, a mischievous grin forming on her lips. "Sebastian, how would you feel about having babies with me?"

"How can you take such a leap in such a short time, after all I've put you through?"

"You're not helping your case, Mr. Mauer." She ran her hands up his arms and linked them behind his neck, stepping in closer. "I remember the feelings we shared; feelings that I know we still have for one another no matter what fool reasons came between us. Yes, we've both changed as well in those years apart, but for the better, I think. We can begin to appreciate one another in an entirely new aspect, and we'll begin to make new memories together. Better memories." She gently touched her lips to his before speaking again. "When I go in, I go all in, Sebastian."

A thousand thoughts ran through his mind, but in the end, the one most clear was having Penelope. He pictured a life with her, a family. A mix of raven-haired beauties and tow-headed hellions who would fill their house. Their home. He pictured forever.

"Penelope, how would you feel about marrying me?"

—

"Yes." Penelope sighed as she sank into Sebastian. His arms came around her and held her tight as he rained kisses atop her head. When she pulled back, she turned around and said, "I believe you were just about to help me with my dress."

"I believe I was." Sebastian leaned forward to kiss the back of her neck before softly whispering, "I will show you every day how much your forgiveness means to me. I will never again take for granted the gift of your love." He pulled the zipper down and parted the material until it fell from her shoulders and slid down her body.

Penelope had no bra or panties on, only the stockings and the boots. She stepped away from the discarded dress and turned to face Sebastian, delighted with his intense gaze.

"You wicked woman. This is all you had on beneath your dress?"

She nodded her head. "Would you mind terribly helping me with the rest?" She watched him move close and kneel down on one knee as he began unzipping her boots. Penelope rested her hands on his shoulders as he lifted one leg then the other to remove them. Sebastian then looked up at her as he slipped his fingers into the waistband of the stockings and slowly rolled them over her hips and down her legs. When he got to her toes, she again lifted each foot in order for him to slip the nylons off.

Penelope stood completely naked before the kneeling Sebastian, his head directly in front of her sex. She should have felt self-conscious and nervous, but a calm washed over her, leaving her with a feeling of rightness unlike any other she'd ever felt. She watched Sebastian lean forward and lift his face, placing a kiss just above the curls at the V of her thighs. As she threaded her fingers through his hair, he moved his tongue from one hip to another before standing.

"You are the most gorgeous creature." He captured her mouth as his hands wound through her hair.

Penelope wrapped her arms around his waist and held on as he began to take her on a sensual journey. He backed her to the bed until her knees hit and he sat her down. Stepping back, he began to undress, tossing his jacket on a nearby chair. He toed off his shoes and unfastened his pants to slide them down his legs. Once he rid himself of everything else, standing naked before her, Penelope had the same thought as him.

"You're gorgeous," she murmured. His toned muscles and sprinkling of chest hair were perfection, and his erection appealed to her so much that she reached out to touch him. Hearing him hiss, she brought her eyes to his face, seeing his control barely restrained.

Sebastian removed her hands from him and leaned forward to kiss her. When he broke from the kiss he told her to lie back. She did, never taking her eyes off of him. He leaned over her, hands on either side of her body as he licked and teased one nipple, then the other. Her eyes closed, and she couldn't help but sigh as his mouth and tongue worked their magic. Her body came alive as currents of desire raced through her. She arched into him and held his head to her chest; loving his attention and how it made her feel.

When he began to kiss down her belly and his hands caressed her ribs, she wiggled beneath him. Then he parted her thighs and his fingers found her most intimate spot beneath her curls. He caressed her, swirling in her moisture. She felt a burning in her core, a building intensity that had a life all its own. As her legs instinctively spread open further, she felt him insert a finger inside her while using his thumb on her sensitive spot. He rubbed and pinched, and it didn't take long until she felt herself explode.

Penelope barely held onto her scream as pleasure overtook her. Wave after wave of ecstasy flooded her entire body.

"You are magnificent," he praised.

He pulled away and closed her legs. Standing above her, he held out his arms and said, "Give me your hands." When she managed to lift her arms, he held her hands and pulled her to a standing position in front of him. They were chest to chest as he branded her mouth with his.

"I want you under the covers," he finally said, leading her around the side of the bed. He pulled back the comforter and sheets, telling her to climb in. "I'll be right back."

Penelope watched him walk to the bathroom, the muscles in his amazing rear flexing with each step. He emerged with a towel in hand and came to the bed. "Let's put this beneath you." He had the towel folded in half and placed it on the bed.

She knew their first time having intercourse would result in bleeding, and he had been conscientious enough to ensure they wouldn't soil the sheets.

"And how will we explain *this* to housekeeping?"

"I plan to throw it out and pay for a new one." He grinned. "Lay back, Penelope," he said gently. "I can't wait another moment to be inside you."

As she lay down on the bed, Sebastian crawled over her, settling between her legs. He kept his weight on his hands and knees, and even without touching, she could feel the heat radiating off of him, stirring her once again. She reached up to touch his chest, running her nails across his taught skin before she lifted herself to kiss him.

Their kisses alone drove her wild. And when he pulled away she could see the animal in him ready to pounce. He held his own erection and moved it up and down her folds, coating the head in her moisture. When he positioned it at her entrance, he kissed her again and then said, "Hold tight. Pleasure will soon follow the pain."

Penelope held his shoulders as he slowly entered, piercing her. The quick stab of pain had her crying out, but as soon as it was there, it was gone, and she began to relax as he held himself still.

"Are you all right?" he asked.

"Excellent." She flexed her hips and felt her insides squeeze, wanting him to move.

Slowly Sebastian sank further into her until it seemed their pelvic bones met. Then he withdrew and did it all over again.

"Ah, you feel so good, so tight around me."

"You fill me up, Sebastian. I love you."

"And I love you." He began to move more rapidly, flexing his hips as well, rubbing her in just the right spot. "I want to feel you come again. I want to feel you squeeze me."

Penelope whimpered and moaned as he moved faster. She scored his flesh with her nails as he thrust deeper, harder; until she ignited. She didn't even try to contain her scream as the pleasure tore through her. Two more thrusts and Sebastian shook from the force of his own climax. Groaning, he collapsed onto her chest before wrapping his arms around her and pulling her in tight. He then rolled them over as they rode out the wondrous feeling together.

She could feel herself pulsing around him as tiny shudders ran through his body. Their skin was slick with perspiration and the smell of their love making scented the air. Lifting her head, she smiled down at the man she loved and kissed him soundly.

"I'm so glad I waited."

"Are you all right?" he asked. A finger feathered her cheek as his other hand gently tickled her back.

"You never need to ask me that again, Sebastian. With you, I'm complete."

"I couldn't have said it better." He lifted the pendant that still hung from her neck and had come to rest on him. "This looks beautiful against your naked flesh. I could get used to this."

"What? Me naked, wearing only jewelry?" She grinned.

"Definitely." After a quick kiss, Sebastian suggested they shower.

Penelope peeled herself away from his alluring body and walked to the bathroom with Sebastian not far behind. They spent the next half hour exploring more of each other's bodies before they finally got clean. Once they were dry and the soiled towel was placed in a bag, Sebastian turned off the lights and they climbed back into bed, snuggling together until sleep came.

Chapter 20

With morning came more tender lovemaking before each showered, and Sebastian headed down to his room for a change of clothes. Penelope met him downstairs for breakfast where they talked about what they wanted to do over the weekend. Sebastian made it known that he wanted to take her shopping for an engagement ring that very day, so they returned to Tiffany's and picked out the perfect one. A round diamond solitaire set in platinum now adorned her hand. Penelope then insisted on purchasing a set of platinum and onyx cuff links for Sebastian – her version of an engagement present.

She snapped a photo of her ring and sent it to Lindsay with the wonderful news. Lindsay instantly texted back that she couldn't wait until Monday to see it, but supposed she'd have to, wishing them a wondrous weekend.

For most of the drizzly afternoon, Penelope and Sebastian explored the vastness of Pike Place Market before settling on dinner at the casual Jasmine Thai Restaurant. While enjoying a variety of dishes, they shared ideas about telling their respective parents of the engagement, as well as planning out the coming weeks. Eventually, they decided that immediate phone calls would be appropriate. While concentrating now on preparing for the performances, later they would plan for an engagement party in May.

Penelope also suggested that they abandon their separate rooms and see if the Fairmont had an executive suite available that they could move into together, providing them with more room. Sebastian thoroughly loved the idea, and when they returned that afternoon from Pike's Market, he spoke with the front desk manager. As luck would have it, a suite was coming available by week's end, so arrangements were made for the consolidation move.

Before heading to Penelope's room, Sebastian stopped by his own to grab the necessary items he'd need for the next few days. Once they locked themselves inside, they made their calls to Bernard and Daphine – both of course were extremely overjoyed – and the couple didn't emerge until Monday morning when it was time to return to rehearsals.

—

The next two weeks were a flurry of activity with them moving in together, the news coming out about their engagement, and preparations for the Symphony's performances.

Unfortunately, LaPelle's condition was taking longer than expected to improve, and he had no choice but to take an extended leave of absence. This gave Sebastian the opportunity to officially become the music director and lead the Symphony until further notice.

—

The days leading up to the performance saw Sebastian and Penelope welcoming Daphine, Bernard, and Gertie to Seattle and to the Fairmont, where they were all able to secure rooms. During a dinner together, there was much discussion about their reunion, the music, and certainly their future.

When asked if Sebastian saw himself staying in Seattle, he said he could envision going anywhere Penelope wanted to go. For the remainder of the season, they would remain at the Fairmont and spend as many weekends as they could up at Sebastian's place on Sinclair Island. He was eager for Penelope to make his house their home. He also dearly missed Samson and Delilah, and Penelope was anxious to make their acquaintance. The dogs were currently staying with a friend of Daphine's while she spent the days in Seattle.

"And of course there's plenty of room at home in San Francisco," Bernard said. "I hope you won't hesitate to return any time you'd like. Daphine, you're welcome as well, should you ever decide you'd like to visit."

"That's very kind of you. I've never been and would love to visit."

"I think you'd enjoy the markets and artisan culture," Gertie added.

"Who knows," Sebastian started, "you may find more outlets for your artistry. Didn't you say you started an account on ETSY?"

"I did!" Daphine's excitement was a pleasure to witness. "I'm selling jewelry and pottery. And, I've begun to dabble in woodworking."

"That's marvelous!" Gertie replied. "Today's world has become something, hasn't it? Why, just the thought of people across the country from one another chatting face-to-face online wasn't anything I thought I'd ever see in my day."

"Exactly! And just last week I had a gal from Europe purchase items from me. Amazing!"

As one day rolled into another, excitement for the performance was building. The symphony's rehearsals had been flawless and filled with an exuberance that rivaled any performance that Sebastian and Penelope had ever been a part of.

Penelope had the opportunity to introduce her father, Gertie, and Daphine to her new friends, Lindsay and Cheryl.

Lindsay happened to be spending much of her free time with Kellen, the guitarist from Euphoria. Although it was early in their relationship, it looked promising, and Penelope was thrilled for her friend.

As for Cheryl, she and Euphoria continued to perform amongst rave reviews, and Cheryl ensured Penelope that she wouldn't miss her debut with the Symphony.

—

The night had finally arrived, and a limousine would be waiting for Sebastian, Penelope, and the others in order to be taken from the Fairmont to Benaroya Hall.

As Sebastian and Penelope were preparing in their suite, Sebastian was completely in awe of Penelope's beauty. She wore a strapless silk gown in royal blue that hugged her bodice and gathered at the waist, with the billowing length of the skirt reaching her ankles. Her diamond heart earrings perfectly matched her heart key pendant, and silver strappy heals completed the outfit.

"You look exquisite," Sebastian said as she twirled in front of him.

"And you look divine," Penelope returned, admiring the black tuxedo with silk lapels, brilliant white shirt, and the cuff links she had gifted him.

"How are you feeling?"

She entered his arms, her hands resting against his chest. "Magnificent. I'd say we're ready."

"We're more than ready." He gave her a quick peck. "I've been thinking. That maybe it's time to give my composition a proper name, like, "Penelope's Song" or "Ode to Penelope". Maybe even revise it."

"Revise it?"

"Give it a happy ending. After all, it was inspired by you, and now that we're back together–"

"I think it's perfect as is. It reflects your feelings and frame of mind at the time. Besides, there are always future compositions that you can dedicate to me." She wiggled her eyebrows at him.

"Hmm, at the risk of sounding cheesy–"

"Oh, but I love it when you do." She grinned.

"Tonight is the start of us making beautiful music together."

Epilogue

Five months later

"Samson, Delilah, lie down, please!"

The two were a bundle of energy, dancing around as Penelope and Sebastian moved around the house, rearranging furniture, and settling a few new pieces in place. Reluctantly, the excited retrievers listened to their master and sought out their beds, plopping down with unmistakable sighs.

Penelope couldn't help but chuckle at their upset. "I think they're actually pouting. Look at their faces." As if knowing they were being talked about, the dogs raised their heads and started to whine. "Oh, you're being silly," Penelope said as she gave each one a head scratch and a quick kiss on their snouts. "You two stay right there for a bit and we'll go for a walk soon enough."

Sebastian only snorted as he continued to push the couch around while Penelope fussed with a side table.

"Don't over-do it," Sebastian warned. "Leave the heavy stuff for me."

"Oh for Heaven's sake, I think I can manage this little table, thank you very much."

The two had taken the month of August – the break that the Symphony took – to make their union official. They had had an intimate wedding ceremony at their home on Sinclair Island to not only celebrate their marriage, but to also celebrate Penelope's pregnancy, which was nearly five months along. She wasn't surprised when their reunion had indeed resulted in a pregnancy, and the two of them couldn't have been happier.

But much to Penelope's exasperation, Sebastian was making sure that she hardly lifted a finger to do anything. While she adored his concern for her, she had to constantly remind him that she wasn't some frail being who had to sit and rest during the entire duration of the pregnancy.

"Women throughout time have endured much more hardship than moving some furniture about."

"Yes, well those women weren't my wife, carrying my child, who will have the most pampered pregnancy that I can provide." Sebastian walked to Penelope and embraced her, careful to keep from pressing into her belly. Her small baby bump looked as if she was only a few months along, but the doctor had assured them that all had been progressing normally with the baby's development.

Penelope looped her arms around her husband's neck and gave him a sound kiss. "And I love that you feel the need to provide such pampering, but it's driving me mad." She gritted her teeth and playfully snarled at him. "I'm not going to break. I've got four more months of this, and I promise to take it easy at the first sign of fatigue."

"You can be sure that I'll see that you do." Sebastian grinned. "Now, are you still up for that walk?" He glanced over her shoulder at the twins. "Because those two are more than ready."

"Yes." She chuckled. "Let's go for that walk." Penelope grabbed a sweater to put on, as their summer had been unseasonably cool. Sebastian whistled for Samson and Delilah who were quickly at the door. Once outside, the dogs leapt off the porch and began running circles in the yard, waiting for their master and mistress. For all their energy, they were well disciplined and never strayed too far ahead.

At five in the evening, there was still plenty of daylight remaining even if the air held a chill. Penelope snuggled into Sebastian's side as the two made their way across the yard and onto the lane that would lead them out to the main road.

"Are you happy here?" Sebastian asked. "It's a far cry from Seattle and San Francisco."

"And that's why I love it," Penelope answered. "While I do enjoy the city, I've come to love it here more. I love the seclusion and the privacy we have. I love the room to do as we please and the ability to have Samson and Delilah. I can see why you had missed them so much. Every time we'd come home for a weekend, only to leave all too soon, I would miss them terribly. They're a treasure."

"*You* are a treasure." He placed a soft kiss on top of her head as they walked. "I am a lucky man to have you back again, and soon, to be welcoming our child into our lives."

"We're both fortunate." They strolled in silence, enjoying the calm of the evening after working non-stop for the past two weeks to make Sebastian's house their home. All too soon they would return to Seattle to begin preparations for the next Symphony's season.

Sebastian had finished out the previous season conducting, and had enjoyed it immensely. It certainly didn't hurt his ego and reputation that his performance was well received; so much so that he was asked to stay on as the music director for the next season due to LaPelle deciding on an early retirement.

After battling with his allergies and a respiratory infection, LaPelle made the decision to move out of Seattle and seek a warmer climate. He and his wife had relocated to Southern Utah, staying for most of the year and returning to the Northwest for the months of July and August. Penelope was delighted that they were able to attend hers and Sebastian's wedding, along with Bernard, Gertie, Daphine, Lindsay and Cheryl. A reception was scheduled to take place in early September once they returned to Seattle, at the urging of Mr. Heitz. It would allow the entire Symphony and the administration to celebrate their union.

Penelope was excited about the upcoming season and the many fabulous performances that were scheduled. If her pregnancy went as planned, the baby would be due just shy of Christmas. She had hoped to continue to perform right up until the birth; again, if all went as planned.

But sometimes nature had other ideas. She would just have to gauge how she felt as time went along.

"You're awfully quiet," Sebastian said softly. "Care to share what's on your mind?"

"Just feeling blessed with my life. I've been thinking about the upcoming season, the birth of the baby, and how it will affect the schedule."

"That's a lot to contemplate." He chuckled. "Are you rethinking taking time off sooner?"

"Absolutely not." She wrinkled her nose at him. "As long as I feel well and my activity poses no threat to our child, I plan to perform right up 'til the birth. And, depending on the schedule, we won't worry about a temporary replacement until November."

"Penelope, are you sure–"

She stopped and faced her husband. "Sebastian, I know you care for me, and your worry is heart-felt, but please, let me do this. If I'm not playing or somehow involved, I'll go crazy and you know it. Now, let's put this subject aside, as we have a visitor."

At the sudden excited barking from Samson and Delilah, Sebastian raised his head to see a vehicle slowly approaching their lane. They both recognized the vehicle as one of the other island's residents, Tamara, who lived near the main dock. The dogs joined Penelope and Sebastian, sitting patiently by the couple's side until the pickup came to a stop. Before greetings could be exchanged, Daphine jumped out of the passenger side, calling out a "hello". That immediately had the dogs racing with excitement towards her.

"Oh my sweet babies, how are you?" Daphine cooed. She bent forward to hug each canine and receive sloppy kisses.

Tamara leaned out of the cab of the truck and said hello as well. "Found this gal hitchin' a ride at the dock. Figured it'd be the neighborly thing to do to bring her 'round to ya." She winked.

"Thank you, Tamara," Sebastian said. He and Penelope approached the truck to welcome his mother. "What a surprise, we weren't expecting you, Mother."

"And that is what's nice about surprises." She straightened and smiled at the couple as she gave them both hugs. "Lucky for me, Tamara was home, or else I'd have had a terrible time juggling my boxes. I hope you don't mind, but I just had a feeling I needed to come see you two."

"Not at all, Daphine, we love your visits," Penelope answered. "I hope everything's all right."

Daphine waved away any concern. "Of course, of course. I've had such a prosperous garden this year, I wanted to come share my bounty and enjoy some time with my two favorite people in the world. Not to mention my two favorite four-legged creatures." With that, she resumed her furious petting of the twins who were more than happy to receive her attention.

"Well, let me just get your things up to the house," Tamara started. "I'll set everything on the porch while you all finish enjoying your walk. Unless you all want a ride, that is."

"No, no, we'll walk back," Daphine said. "Give us all more time to stretch our legs. And thank you so much, Tamara. You be sure to take some jars of that jam I told you about. There's plenty to go around."

"Thank you much, Daph, I'll do just that."

Everyone backed away from the vehicle so Tamara could head to the house. Daphine fell in step with Penelope and Sebastian as the dogs raced behind the truck, keeping a safe distance.

"So how's my favorite daughter-in-law doing?" Daphine looped her arm around Penelope's right arm, as her left was still holding hands with Sebastian.

Penelope chuckled. "Well, as your *only* daughter-in-law, I'm feeling marvelous. Sebastian and I have got the house arranged pretty much to our liking, and we were just beginning to discuss the upcoming season."

"Ah, I can only imagine that conversation." Her sarcastic tone didn't go unnoticed by her son.

"Is that so?" Sebastian asked.

With a little grin, Daphine continued. "Well, yes. You, my dear son, probably want to coddle and pamper your wife, thinking she shouldn't over-do it. And while Penelope adores your concern, she's probably ready to club you."

Penelope couldn't help but burst with laughter. "While I wouldn't go so far as to club him, I have already made him aware that I know my limitations. And, while his concern *is* adorable," Penelope gave Sebastian a quick peck on the cheek, "enough is enough."

"Well, you can't blame me," Sebastian said defensively.

"Of course not," both Penelope and Daphine said, eliciting more laughter.

"Darling, at least you care." Penelope cooed.

"Indeed," Daphine stated. "Now, I've got dinner all planned, so both of you can relax this evening and let me take care of you." They approached the house just a Tamara had turned around and was making her way out.

Waves and good-byes were exchanged before Sebastian led the ladies up the porch. As the dogs continued to play in the yard, Daphine and her son grabbed boxes to cart inside while Penelope held the door.

"This is very thoughtful of you," Penelope said as the last of the items were placed in the kitchen. "We always look forward to all that you have to share, Daphine."

"I bought fresh salmon at the market and I have plenty of greens from my garden. I also made fresh bread and there's berry jam to go with it."

"Sounds wonderful, Mother, thank you."

"You're absolutely welcome. Now, you two, go, while I put everything together." She gestured playfully as if to shoo them out of the kitchen. "It won't take long to sear the salmon. I'll call you when it's ready."

"I'll put out some food and water for Samson and Delilah," Sebastian said. He turned to Penelope. "I'll join you shortly." With a quick kiss, he went to the pantry to retrieve the dog's dry kibble. Once back out on the porch, the dogs hurried to his side, knowing it was their dinner time.

Penelope watched with affection, feeling as if life couldn't get any better. Daphine joined her side and gave her a hug.

"I'm so happy that you two found one another again. I see only good things in the future."

Penelope leaned her head into Daphine's and sighed. "Life is a blessing."

"That it is," Daphine said as she pulled away, telling Penelope to go sit. "While I won't turn into my son and insist that you rest day in and day out, I'll just tell you to get it while you can."

"Thank you." Penelope kissed her cheek and left the kitchen, walking to the front room. She eyed the cozy area as contentment washed over her. She and Sebastian had picked up a few pieces of furniture and embellishments to fill some of the empty space, making it warm and inviting; making it their home. Taking a seat on the couch, she kicked her legs up by her side and rested her head on a pillow. Closing her eyes, she was fast asleep before she realized.

—

Sebastian entered the living room, finding Penelope asleep on the couch. She looked more beautiful to him every day, and he thanked God that he found his way back into her life and her heart.

While trying not to disturb her, he cuddled up beside her and kicked his feet up on the coffee table. Taking in his surroundings, he marveled at how quickly Penelope had made his house, their home. He was already used to the changes as little additions here and there seemed as if they'd been in place all along. It was Penelope's presence above all that filled the space and filled his heart. Now, he couldn't imagine a life without her, and thankfully, he wouldn't have to.

Closing his eyes, he too, fell asleep.

Sebastian slowly opened his eyes at the gentle prodding against his leg, seeing Delilah resting her head on his thigh. When he could fully focus, he looked at the clock on the wall and saw that two hours had passed. Looking to his right, he saw that Penelope was still asleep and a blanket had been draped across her. Still not wanting to disturb her, he gently lifted himself off the couch as Delilah followed. Samson was lounging on his bed, snoring. As he made his way into the kitchen, he noticed a note on the table. He picked it up and read his mother's words.

My dear sleepyheads, I didn't have the heart to wake you, so I put dinner aside. Now don't think that I'm upset; we can visit one another any time. It was just so nice to see you both. I'm sure Delilah watched over you, and she'll rest when she's ready ☺

I rode one of the bikes to the dock; I'll leave it with Tamara.

I'll see you soon enough; so in the meantime, enjoy one another.

Love you! Love, your mother xo

Sebastian saw the covered basket of bread with several bottles of jam beside it on the table. In the refrigerator, he saw the wrapped salmon and the bowl of salad. Smiling at his mother's thoughtfulness, he'd be sure to call her later.

He turned at the sound of shuffling feet, and saw that Penelope and Samson were walking towards him.

"I missed dinner, didn't I?"

"Actually, we both did." He grinned. "I came in and found you asleep, so I sat next to you, and apparently slept as well."

"And Daphine?"

Sebastian held up the note for Penelope to read. "Oh, I'm sorry."

"No need to be. She even said so." He kissed her forehead. "Are you hungry?"

"Famished." When she smiled, it took his breath away.

"Let's wash up and eat then."

They thoroughly enjoyed Daphine's offerings, and after tidying the kitchen, they decided to sit out on the porch in order to watch the day turn into night.

A short time later, Sebastian watched Penelope try to stifle a yawn as she suggested they go to bed.

"I'll gladly take you up on that offer. I'll take care of the twins and be in soon."

As Penelope nodded and went inside, Sebastian allowed the dogs to take care of their nightly business before ushering them inside. They immediately went to their beds and happily plopped down.

"Good night, you two," he called out before making his way to his and Penelope's bedroom.

After seeing to his needs, he undressed to his boxers and joined Penelope in bed. Pulling back the covers, he was happily surprised to see his wife naked, a wicked smile forming on her lips.

"You, my dear husband, are overdressed."

"Is that so?" He took in the sight of his beautiful wife with her tiny rounded belly and her firm breasts, already plumping due to the pregnancy. He could see what people meant when they said a pregnant lady glowed. Penelope was stunning.

"Tell me you're not going to just stand there and stare?" she questioned with a teasing smile.

"Are you sure, I mean, the ba–"

"Sebastian," she warned. "It's perfectly safe. The doctor said so. In bed, now," she commanded.

"Absolutely, m'lady." Sebastian smirked as he quickly removed his boxers and joined her in bed. Penelope wasted no time by crawling on top of his body and kissing him sweetly. She felt like heaven as she rested against him. He took the kiss deeper, feasting on her mouth while his hands roamed down her back to her behind. Giving her a squeeze, he was delighted with her squeal, sparking more excitement in him.

His erection strained against her mound, and Penelope took that moment to grind her pelvis into his.

"You truly are a wicked woman."

"I am *your* wicked woman." She nipped at his mouth. "And I plan to show you just how wicked I can be."

Penelope sat up as her hand caressed his length before guiding him to her entrance. Ever so slowly, she seated herself upon him, and it took all his control not to begin a fierce rhythm of pumping himself to orgasm. She felt exquisite as her insides clenched around him; her own ecstasy evident on her gorgeous face.

"Penelope, you are driving me mad," he said through clenched teeth.

"Is that so?" She continued to tease. "Well, we can't have that." She positioned her hands on his shoulders and began to rise then descend; rise and descend.

He allowed her to set the rhythm, knowing that they'd both be rewarded soon. With one hand, Sebastian massaged a breast before plucking the pebbled nipple. With the other, he thumbed the bundle of nerves at the top of her sex, groaning as he felt her tighten.

"Oh, Sebastian, please don't stop." Her ecstasy-filled voice a raspy plea.

"I won't if you won't," he managed to say.

And with that she began to move faster and harder as he stroked her to orgasm; his soon following. When she collapsed on his chest, he wrapped his arms around her and held tight, keeping them connected.

"I don't want to move," she whispered.

"Then don't."

Tenderly, he trailed his fingertips up and down her back, loving the feel of her smooth, soft skin. A few moments later, she lifted herself up, saying she had to go to the bathroom. Sebastian marveled at his good fortune as he watched her leave the bed.

"I love you," he called to her.

Penelope stopped and turned to him. She was a vision with her wild curls, her sleepy smile, and her beautifully round tummy. Not to mention the look of being completely sated from their lovemaking.

"And I love you," she returned softly.

Once she had finished and returned to bed, Sebastian welcomed her into his arms once again. As they cuddled, his hand automatically went to her abdomen, lightly running his fingers across her smooth yet stretched skin. His thoughts wondered at the child they had created.

As if reading his mind, she said, "This child will be perfect, and I can't wait to welcome him, or her, into our world."

"My thoughts exactly. I am so blessed." He couldn't think it or say it enough.

"We both are." She lifted her face to kiss him. "Now, let's get some sleep. You wore me out." She yawned.

"I think you had a part in that as well," he teased.

"That I did. And I'll gladly do it again. In the morning," she added with a grin.

He kissed her soundly before tightening his hold on her, knowing that this time, he'd never let her go.

The End

View other Black Rose Writing titles at www.blackrosewriting.com/books and use promo code **PRINT** to receive a **20% discount** when purchasing.

BLACK ROSE writing™

Please condiser leaving a review; Amazon, Goodreads, or wherever you choose

CPSIA information can be obtained
at www.ICGtesting.com
Printed in the USA
FSOW03n0410280717
36693FS